Will You Marry Me?

Michael Gordon

Published by MG Books, 2024.

This is a work of fiction. Similarities to real people, places, or events are entirely coincidental.

WILL YOU MARRY ME?

First edition. November 1, 2024.

Copyright © 2024 Michael Gordon.

ISBN: 979-8227300850

Written by Michael Gordon.

Chapter 1

Zayden sat comfortably in the studio, his dark skinned, muscular frame was relaxed in the chair. He was wearing a long sleeve blue shirt, with a pair of skinny black jeans. His tattoos were peeking out from beneath the cuffs. The interview with Emma Rand, the reality tv show producer, was underway. Zayden's deep voice resonated through the room as he spoke about his willingness to open up his life to the cameras for the popular tv show known as *Will You Marry Me?* He had a certain charm that came naturally to him, a result of his years as a popular football player and now a beloved teacher in the community.

"So, Zayden, how do you feel about having cameras follow your every move?" Emma's voice was warm and inviting, her plus-sized figure exuding a sense of comfort and trust.

"I'm cool with it, Emma," Zayden replied with a broad smile. *"I mean, I'm used to being in the spotlight, you know, from my football days. Besides, I think it's time I let someone else into my world. I'm ready to find the one."*

Emma's eyes sparkled with excitement. *"That's fantastic! And what about the woman you're hoping to meet? Do you have a particular type in mind?"*

Zayden leaned back, his broad shoulders moving with the motion. *"Well, physically, I don't have a specific preference. As a black man, I've always been attracted to black women, but I'm open to anyone. It's more about the connection, you know? I want someone who's kind, outgoing, and maybe a little adventurous. Someone who can keep up with my sense of humor and isn't afraid to try new things."*

Emma nodded, making a few notes on her clipboard. *"That's wonderful. And are you prepared for the idea of marrying someone you've never met before? This show is all about taking a leap of faith. You will be marrying some sight unseen. You won't know what they look like or any of their features or traits. Are you okay with that?"*

A hint of nervousness flashed across Zayden's face, but he quickly composed himself. *"Yeah, I am. I mean, I've been on the dating scene for a while, and it's getting old. I'm ready to settle down, and if this is what it takes, I'm all for it. Besides, I trust your team to find me someone amazing."*

Emma beamed, her brunette hair framing her face as she leaned forward. *"Welcome to the show, Zayden. I have a good feeling about this. I think we can find you the perfect match."*

Zayden's smile widened, his white teeth flashing. *"Thanks, Emma. I appreciate the opportunity. I'm excited to see who I'll be sharing my life with."*

As Zayden's interview concluded, an hour later, the crew prepared for the next participant, Sabrina. Her entrance into the studio was a stark contrast to Zayden's relaxed demeanor.

She walked in, her long dark hair cascading down her back, and took a seat, her curvy figure slightly hunched as if she was trying to make herself smaller. Sabrina was in a pair of jeans and a silk white blouse. Emma noticed the intricate tattoo peeking out from under her blouse and the glint of a bellybutton ring, a hidden rebellion beneath her conservative appearance.

"Sabrina, it's lovely to meet you. How are you feeling about the cameras?" Emma's voice was gentle, sensing the young woman's nervousness.

Sabrina's almond-shaped eyes darted around the room, taking in the camera crew. *"It's a bit strange, to be honest. I'm not used to being the center of attention."*

"Well, we're here to make you feel comfortable. Why don't you tell me a little about yourself and why you decided to join the show, Will You Marry Me?" Emma encouraged her.

Sabrina's voice was soft, almost a whisper. *"I'm turning thirty soon, and my parents have been pressuring me to get married. They want to set me up with someone from our Asian community, but I... I want to find my own partner. I'm tired of being controlled, and I thought this might be a way to take charge of my love life."*

It felt weird to finally admit her true feelings, especially on national television, but Sabrina was tried of living underneath her father's thumb

Emma nodded in understanding. *"That's a brave decision. And what are you looking for in a husband?"*

"I want someone who can help me come out of my shell. I'm shy, and I've always been the quiet one. I want someone outgoing, someone who can show me new experiences and maybe even teach me how to dance," she added with a hint of embarrassment. *"I've always liked men with tattoos, maybe a bit muscular. I don't want someone controlling, that's for sure."*

Emma's eyes lit up. *"That's wonderful! And you're open to different races, backgrounds? We want to find you someone who complements you perfectly."*

"Yes, absolutely. I mean, I've always had a preference for white men, but it's more about the connection, like you said. I just want someone who loves me for who I am." Sabrina's voice grew more confident as she spoke.

"Perfect! Sabrina, I think you're going to have a wonderful journey on this show. Just remember, you'll be marrying a complete stranger, and you'll live together for three months. Are you ready for this adventure?"

Sabrina took a deep breath, her eyes determined. *"I am. I want to find love, and I don't care if it's with someone I've never met before. I'm ready to take a chance."*

Emma smiled warmly, her maternal instincts kicking in. *"Then welcome to Will You Marry Me, Sabrina. I have a feeling your life is about to change in the most wonderful way."*

Sabrina smiled back and prayed that it would. She felt like she was crazy for putting her love life in the public spotlight, but she was ready for a change. She was ready for love. She just prayed that her unknown match felt the same.

Chapter 2

The evening air buzzed with excitement and anticipation as the four bachelors of the hit reality show 'Will You Marry Me?' gathered at a trendy bar in Virginia Beach. It was the night before their big day, the day they would meet their potential brides, and the anticipation was palpable.

Zayden Moss, Billy Twine, Josh Hawkins, and Xavier Washington, each with their unique personalities and backgrounds, engaged in lively banter, their voices mingling with the clinking of glasses and the soft murmurs of the crowd.

Zayden, a former college football star turned math teacher, stood out with his muscular build, tattoos, and infectious smile. His deep voice carried across the table as he joked with his fellow bachelors, his laughter filling the space. He was the life of the party, a charismatic presence that drew people in. Next to him, Billy Twine, a former college basketball player and successful businessman, exuded an air of confidence and charm. With his model-like looks and square jaw, he was the epitome of a ladies' man, his blue eyes scanning the room with an air of entitlement.

On the other side of the table, Josh, a skinny and unassuming black man, kept mostly to himself. His glasses slipped down his nose as he quietly sipped his drink, his eyes darting around the room with a hint of nervousness. Josh, a fantasy writer and book editor, had joined the show hoping to find a kindred spirit, a geeky wife who shared his love for books and comics. He was the introvert among the group, his quiet demeanor contrasting sharply with the others.

Across from Josh sat Xavier, a man of faith and conviction. He was a big, burly man with a warm smile and a gentle spirit. Xavier's faith was his guiding light, and he was determined to find a wife who shared his devotion to Christ. He believed in the power of love and destiny, and his optimism was infectious, making him a beloved figure among the crew.

As the night wore on, the conversation inevitably turned to the topic of women. Each bachelor had their own idea of the perfect wife, and the discussion became animated. Billy, ever the ladies' man, declared his preference for trophy wives, preferably blonde and beautiful. He boasted about his wealth and success, claiming that he wanted a woman who would be a status symbol by his side. His arrogance was evident, and the others exchanged glances, knowing that Billy's attitude might not sit well with some.

"I'm not looking for a trophy, but a partner," Zayden chimed in, his deep voice commanding attention. *"I want a woman whose kind, adventurous, and not afraid to speak her mind. Someone who'll challenge me and keep life interesting."* Zayden's eyes sparkled with enthusiasm, and Emma, the show's producer, nodded in agreement, in the background behind the camera's bright light, understanding the importance of compatibility.

"For me, it's all about finding someone who shares my passions," Josh said, his voice soft but determined. *"I want a wife who'll spend Sundays reading comics with me and discuss the latest fantasy novels. Someone who gets my love for the nerdy side of life."* His words were met with smiles, as the others appreciated his honesty and desire for a genuine connection. Xavier, with a warm smile, added, *"I pray for a God-fearing woman, someone who'll walk with me in faith and raise a family together. I want a black queen who'll be the heart of our home, a woman of strength and love."* His words resonated with the group, reminding them that love and marriage were about more than just physical attraction.

As the night progressed, Emma, guided the conversation between the men, ensuring the cameras captured every moment. She understood the importance of these initial interactions, knowing they would set the tone for the rest of the show. The producers, ever mindful of creating engaging content, encouraged the bachelors to share their thoughts and feelings, capturing the raw emotions that made reality TV so compelling.

Leaving the bar, the Billy, Josh, and Zayden decided to continue the night at a nearby strip club, a decision that sparked excitement and hesitation in equal measure. Xavier on the other hand wanted no part of the strip club as he viewed the establishment as a den of sin and lust. Instead, he decided to call it an early night, leaving the three bachelors by themselves.

At the strip club, Billy was in his element, flashing his charming smile at the dancers and reveling in the attention. He convinced one of the women, a sultry redhead, to leave with him, and they disappeared into the night, leaving the others shaking their heads in amusement.

Zayden, however, was approached by a stunning woman with long dark hair and piercing green eyes. She ran her fingers along his tattooed arm, her touch sending shivers down his spine. *"You're a handsome one,"* she purred, her breath hot against his ear. *"How about you and I have some private time?"*

Zayden, despite his attraction, politely declined. He had committed to the show and was determined to see it through. *"Thank you, but I'm here for something different tonight,"* he replied, his voice firm yet gentle. The woman, sensing his resolve, smiled and moved on, leaving Zayden feeling a mix of relief and anticipation.

As the night drew to a close, Josh and Zayden made their way back to the hotel, their heads buzzing with excitement and anticipation. Zayden, in particular, felt a surge of adrenaline as he entered his room. He knew that tomorrow would change his life, and he was eager to meet the woman who might become his wife.

He paced around the room, his mind racing with thoughts of the unknown. He wondered what she would look like, what her personality would be, and if they would have that elusive spark that could ignite a flame. Zayden had always been a romantic at heart, despite his tough exterior. He believed in love and the power of connection, and he hoped that this experiment would lead him to something extraordinary.

As he prepared for bed, Zayden's thoughts drifted to his past relationships. He had dated casually, enjoying the freedom and excitement of the dating scene in Virginia Beach. But deep down, he yearned for something more meaningful, a connection that would last. Zayden had always been a bit of a rebel, a trait that sometimes clashed with his parents' traditional values. They had raised him in a Christian household, and while he respected their faith, he had chosen a different path.

His time as a college athlete had been a whirlwind, with the spotlight and adoration of fans. But the transition to a regular life had been challenging. Zayden found himself struggling financially, often living paycheck to paycheck. His love for travel and experiences often left him with little savings, and he knew his credit score reflected his impulsive nature. However, Zayden was determined to make a change, and he saw this reality show as a chance to start fresh.

As he drifted off to sleep, Zayden's mind painted a picture of the woman he hoped to meet. He envisioned a beautiful, confident black woman, someone who would challenge and inspire him. He wanted a partner who would understand his playful side, but also appreciate his desire for a stable future. Zayden knew that finding love on a reality show was a gamble, but he was ready to take that chance, ready to open his heart to the possibility of something extraordinary.

Meanwhile, in another part of the hotel, Emma Rand, the show's producer, was busy reviewing footage and making final preparations. She was a veteran in the reality TV world, having worked on numerous successful shows. Emma's passion for storytelling and her keen eye for detail had made her a respected figure in the industry. She believed in the power of love and human connection, and she worked tirelessly to create an environment where genuine relationships could flourish.

As she scrolled through the footage of the bachelors, Emma couldn't help but feel a sense of excitement. She knew that each man brought something unique to the table, and she was eager to see how their journeys would unfold. Emma had a soft spot for love stories, and she hoped that this season would deliver on the promise of romance and adventure.

The night air carried a hint of salt from the nearby beach, and the sound of distant laughter and music filled the air. Virginia Beach was alive with possibilities, and tomorrow, four lives would be forever changed. As Emma prepared for the big day, she couldn't help but wonder what fate had in store for Zayden, Billy, Josh, and Xavier. The show's premise was a bold one, but Emma believed in the power of taking chances, and she was determined to make this season unforgettable.

Little did they know, the journey ahead would be filled with surprises, heartaches, and moments of pure joy. 'Will You Marry Me?' was about to become the talk of the nation, and these four bachelors were about to embark on a rollercoaster ride of emotions, all in the name of finding their true loves. The stage was set, and the show was ready to begin, leaving the audience wondering who would find love and who would be left heartbroken.

Chapter 3

The anticipation of meeting their potential husbands had brought the four bachelorettes together, each with their unique personalities and desires. Sabrina, Brittney, Victoria, and Yolanda sat in a trendy restaurant in the heart of Virginia Beach, their every move captured by the ever-present cameras and the show's eager producers. The atmosphere buzzed with excitement and nerves as they indulged in a lavish dinner, courtesy of the show's production team.

Brittney Gamble, the stunning brunette with model-like features, couldn't help but feel giddy. She had joined the show for the chance to find a wealthy husband who would pamper her, and she was determined to make the most of this opportunity. With her grey eyes sparkling, she declared, *"I'm looking for a man who can sweep me off my feet and provide me with a life of luxury. I want someone who can take me on adventures and spoil me with gifts."* Her ditzy nature charmed the producers, who saw her as a potential fan favorite.

Sabrina, listened intently to her fellow bachelorettes, her almond-shaped eyes revealing a hint of curiosity. As she sipped her fruit cocktail, she shared, *"I'm not sure what my ideal man looks like, but I want someone who understands my need for independence. Someone who can bring out my fun side without pressuring me."* She secretly hoped to find a white man, drawn to their allure, but she was open to all possibilities.

Victoria Stevens, the nerdy redhead, adjusted her glasses, her green eyes shining with determination. *"For me, it's all about the mind. I want a man who can challenge me intellectually. Someone who understands my passion for computers and shares my love for fantasy novels."* Victoria's preference for personality over physical traits made her stand out among the group. She didn't care much for appearances, but she knew that her unique interests might narrow down her options.

Yolanda Green, the curvy black woman with a commanding presence, spoke with confidence. *"I'm seeking a God-fearing man who will guide me on my spiritual journey. I want someone who shares my faith and can keep me on the path of righteousness. And of course, he needs to be black, handsome and strong."* Yolanda's words were laced with a sense of entitlement, and she made no apologies for her preferences.

As the evening progressed, the women discussed their ideal dates, favorite foods, and even their dislikes. Sabrina cringed at the mention of dancing, her face turning slightly pink. She had never been comfortable with it, especially in public. Sensing her discomfort, Brittney and Yolanda, both extroverted and lively, decided to tease her. *"Oh, come on, Sabrina! Dancing is so much fun. How can you not enjoy it?"* Brittney asked, her playful tone filling the air.

Yolanda chimed in, *"Yeah, you should let loose a little. It's good to let your hair down, especially before your big day."*

Sabrina shifted uncomfortably in her seat, her long dark hair cascading over her shoulders. *"I just... I'm not very good at it, and I feel awkward. I prefer to watch from the sidelines."* Her voice was soft, almost apologetic.

"Nonsense!" Brittney exclaimed. *"We'll teach you! Come on, girls, let's go to a club and show Sabrina how it's done."*

Before Sabrina could protest, the group was whisked away by the show's producers to a nearby dance club, the cameras following their every move. The pulsating music and vibrant atmosphere greeted them as they entered, the club's energy contrasting with Sabrina's reserved nature.

Yolanda and Brittney, full of enthusiasm, immediately made their way to the dance floor, their bodies moving effortlessly to the beat. Sabrina stood by the edge, feeling like a fish out of water. She observed the dancers, her eyes widening as she witnessed Yolanda's boldness.

Yolanda, caught up in the music, began dancing with a tall, muscular black man. As the song progressed, their moves became more intimate, and to Sabrina's surprise, they started kissing passionately. Shocked, Sabrina averted her eyes, feeling a mix of embarrassment and curiosity. *Is this what reality TV is all about?* she wondered. *Am I ready for this kind of exposure?*

As the night wore on, Sabrina's thoughts drifted to her potential husband. *What if he's as wild as Yolanda?* she pondered. *Will he understand my hesitations and help me overcome them?* She knew that by signing up for the show, she had agreed to step out of her comfort zone, but witnessing Yolanda's behavior made her question the extent of the challenges she might face.

Meanwhile, Brittney and Yolanda, unaware of Sabrina's inner turmoil, continued to dance and flirt with various men. Victoria, sensing Sabrina's discomfort, joined her at the edge of the dance floor.

"Don't worry, Sabrina," Victoria said, her voice calm and reassuring. *"Not everyone is as extroverted as Yolanda. I'm not much of a dancer either. We can find other ways to have fun without being the center of attention."*

Sabrina smiled gratefully at Victoria, feeling a sense of camaraderie with the nerdy programmer. She realized that perhaps the show would bring her more than just a husband; it might also gift her with friendships and the courage to embrace new experiences.

As the night drew to a close, the bachelorettes made their way back to their luxurious accommodations, provided by the show. Sabrina, exhausted yet exhilarated, lay in her bed, her thoughts swirling. She knew that the journey ahead would be filled with unexpected twists and turns, but she was determined to find her version of happiness, even if it meant stepping into uncharted territory.

Chapter 4

The sun shone brightly over Virginia Beach, its rays reflecting off the ocean waves and creating a picturesque backdrop for the unusual wedding ceremony. In a hotel conference room transformed into a stunning wedding venue, Zayden and Sabrina stood at the altar, blindfolded, their hearts racing with anticipation and nerves. This was it—the moment they had been waiting for, the moment they would finally see their future spouses.

Emma stood nearby next to the multiple cameras in the room evaluating the upcoming scene. She smiled taking in the elegant white chairs, the beautiful floral arrangements, and the soft blue accents that adorned the space. The oceanfront view through the large bay windows added to the serenity of the setting, making the wedding romantic.

Zayden, with his muscular build and confident demeanor, felt a surge of excitement mixed with trepidation. He had always been a risk-taker, but this was a whole new level of adventure. He could feel the silk of the blindfold on his eyes. It felt weird being walked down the aisle by the producers unable to see. Zayden's heart pounded in his chest, a contrast to his usual laid-back attitude. He wondered who his bride would be, hoping that they would have an instant connection and understanding. Meanwhile, Sabrina stood beside him, a vision of beauty and nervous energy. Her long, dark hair cascaded down her back, and her curvy figure was accentuated by her exquisite wedding gown. She felt like a princess, yet her mind was a whirlwind of thoughts and doubts. Sabrina had always been a private person, and the idea of marrying a stranger, especially in front of a national audience, was overwhelming.

Curious on what the parents expected of their son and daughter, Emma told the cameramen to focus on a few shots of the couple's parents. Emma saw Sabrina's parents, seated in the front row, their faces a mixture of worry and disappointment. Based on the interviews with Sabrina, Emma had no doubt that they had hoped their daughter would find a traditional Korean partner, but instead she is marrying a black man which Emma could tell bothered the Sabrina's father.

Looking at Zayden's family, it was hard to get a read on them. They appeared happy, but Emma questioned if it was genuine or just for the show.

As the ceremony commenced, the officiant's voice echoed through the room, *"Today, we gather to celebrate the union of two souls, brought together by fate and the power of love."* Zayden and Sabrina held hands, their palms sweating slightly as they felt the weight of the moment. The officiant continued, *"Zayden and Sabrina, you have chosen to take a leap of faith, to embark on a journey of discovery and connection. Today, you will see each other for the first time, and I hope you find in each other the love and companionship you seek."*

With those words, the officiant signaled for the couple to remove their blindfolds. Zayden's fingers trembled as he untied the silk scarf covering his eyes. He blinked, adjusting to the light, and then his gaze locked with Sabrina's. Her eyes, a deep almond shape, were wide with surprise, and her full lips parted slightly, revealing a hint of disbelief. Zayden's breath caught in his throat as he took in her beauty, her delicate features, and the hint of a rebellious spirit in her expression.

Sabrina, in turn, was stunned by the man standing before her. Zayden's muscular physique and handsome face were not what she had expected. She had envisioned a different type of partner, someone more conservative and perhaps more in line with her parents' wishes. But there was an undeniable spark in his eyes, a warmth that seemed to reach out to her. She noticed his tattoos, the intricate designs on his arms and the hint of a larger piece on his neck, hidden by his tuxedo.

His diamond earrings added an edge to his appearance, and she found herself drawn to his unique style.

As they stood there, mesmerized by each other, the room seemed to fade away. The cameras, the audience, and even their own doubts became distant as they shared an intimate moment of connection. Zayden's heart raced, and he felt a surge of protectiveness towards Sabrina. He wanted to shield her from the world, to be the one to help her break free from her shell. In that instant, he knew he would do everything in his power to make this marriage work, to show her that taking a chance on love could lead to something extraordinary.

Sabrina, too, felt a rush of emotions. She had always been reserved, but there was something about Zayden that made her want to let go of her inhibitions. His smile, warm and inviting, seemed to promise adventure and a life less ordinary. She thought of her parents and their expectations, and for the first time, she felt a sense of rebellion stir within her. She wanted to prove to them and to herself that she could make her own choices, even if they didn't always align with tradition.

The officiant cleared his throat, breaking the spell that had enveloped the couple. *"Do you, Zayden Moss, take Sabrina Chun as your lawfully wedded wife, to have and to hold, from this day forward, for better or for worse, for richer or for poorer, in sickness and in health, until death do you part?"*

Zayden's voice was steady as he replied, *"I do."* His eyes never left Sabrina's, and he felt a sense of determination to make this work, to be the partner she needed.

The officiant turned to Sabrina, *"And do you, Sabrina Chun, take Zayden Moss as your lawfully wedded husband, to have and to hold, from this day forward, for better or for worse, for richer or for poorer, in sickness and in health, until death do you part?"*

Sabrina's voice trembled slightly, but she answered with conviction, *"I do."* She looked into Zayden's eyes, and in that moment, she felt a glimmer of hope, a promise of a future filled with love and laughter.

With the exchange of vows and rings, the couple sealed their commitment with a kiss. Zayden's lips were gentle yet passionate, and Sabrina responded with a hunger she didn't know she possessed and deepened the kiss between her and the stranger that was now her husband. The audience erupted into cheers and applause, celebrating the union of two strangers who had just taken a giant leap of faith.

As the newlyweds walked down the aisle, hand in hand, they couldn't help but feel a sense of excitement and trepidation. Zayden whispered to Sabrina, *"We're in this together. Let's show them what we're made of."* Sabrina smiled, feeling a surge of confidence in her new husband's words.

Chapter 5

As the newlyweds, Zayden and Sabrina, found themselves alone in a secluded area of the luxurious hotel, they couldn't help but feel a mix of excitement and nervousness. The wedding ceremony had been a whirlwind, and now they were finally able to steal a moment for themselves, away from the prying eyes of their friends and family in the bustling crowd. However, they couldn't rid themselves of the camera crew. They knew being on the show their actions would be viewed at every second.

The hotel had arranged a private room for the couple, complete with a cozy seating area, a bottle of champagne on ice, and a breathtaking view of the ocean. It was the perfect setting for them to get to know each other better and celebrate their unique union.

Zayden, always the charismatic one, took charge of the moment. With a mischievous grin, he popped the cork of the champagne bottle, causing a loud pop that startled Sabrina. She let out a small squeal, her eyes widening with surprise. *"Whoa, easy there!"* she exclaimed, her heart racing. Zayden laughed, his deep voice filling the room with warmth. *"Sorry, babe. I couldn't resist. We should celebrate our marriage, right?"*

"Babe?" She giggled. *"Did we already enter the pet name stage of our relationship?"*

"Yeah, you don't mind, do you?"

"No, I like it." Sabrina smiled, her nervousness melting away as she took in Zayden's playful demeanor. Her hands trembled as she, reaching for a champagne flute. Their finger met and there was an electric connection

between them. There was no denying that there was a physical attraction between the two as Sabrina shuddered, taking a deep breath. Zayden poured the bubbly liquid, the golden bubbles dancing in the glass. They clinked their glasses together, the sound echoing in the quiet room. *"To us,"* Zayden said, his eyes locking with Sabrina's. *"To taking a leap of faith and finding love in the most unexpected way."*

They sipped their champagne, the sweet liquid tickling their taste buds. As they sat on the plush couch, Sabrina's curiosity about her new husband grew. She knew they had exchanged some basic information during the ceremony, but now, she wanted to delve deeper and truly understand the man she had just married. *"So, Zayden, tell me more about yourself. You mentioned you were a college football player. Which school did you go to?"*

Zayden's face lit up as he recalled his glory days. *"I went to North Carolina University. It was a great experience, and I loved every minute of it. I played running back, and I still hold the record for the most rushing yards in a single season."* He flexed his muscular arms, a proud smile on his face.

Sabrina's eyes widened in recognition. *"Oh, I remember you! I went to Virginia University, and we were rivals. I attended a game where you scored two touchdowns. You were incredible. I even thought you might go pro."*

Zayden's smile faltered slightly, and he took a sip of champagne. *"I tried, but it didn't work out. I wasn't quite good enough. After college, I became a math teacher and started coaching football and wrestling at a local high school. I love working with kids and teaching them the game."*

Sabrina's heart warmed at his words. *"That's amazing! I work with kids too. I'm an ER nurse at the pediatric hospital. It's challenging but so rewarding."*

Zayden's eyes sparkled with admiration. *"You're a nurse? That's incredible."*

"I'm glad you think so, my parents aren't particularly happy with my job. My dad is a surgeon and wanted me to go down the same career path, but I failed med school and became a nurse instead."

"Nurses are still important. You are doing a good thing, especially with kids. You should be proud."

Sabrina smirked and brushed a stray hair behind her ear. She felt a stray shiver up her spine wondering how she could be falling for a man she just met. She giggled and playfully slapped his thigh, *"And you went to my rival school? I guess this marriage is off to an interesting start."* He chuckled, his dimples appearing as he grinned.

Sabrina blushed, feeling a strange mix of embarrassment and excitement. *"Well, you're definitely not who I imagined marrying. I mean, you're not my usual type."*

"And what type is that?" Zayden asked, leaning forward, his eyes full of curiosity.

Sabrina felt her cheeks grow warmer. *"Well, I usually prefer men who are a bit more... conservative, I guess. But I find you attractive, Zayden. I like your tattoos and piercings. They suit you."*

Zayden's grin widened, and he leaned back, crossing his arms over his chest. *"Oh, so you like a bad boy, huh? I'm flattered. And for the record, I find you incredibly attractive too. You're stunning, and there's something about you that draws me in."*

Sabrina's heart fluttered at his words. *"Really? What is it?"*

Zayden's gaze traveled down her body, taking in her curves and the way her dark hair cascaded over her shoulders. *"I like everything about you, but I'm especially curious about those tattoos and piercings you mentioned earlier. Do you have any more hidden surprises?"*

Sabrina felt her cheeks flush even more. *"Well, I have a belly button ring and a small tattoo on my lower back. I got them in college, but my parents don't know about them. It's kind of my little secret."*

Zayden's eyes lit up with mischief. *"A rebel, huh? I like that. But now, thanks to the cameras, your parents know about your little secrets!"*

Realization dawned on Sabrina's face, and she laughed, covering her mouth with her hand. *"Oh no! I didn't even think about that. Sorry, Mom and Dad,"* she said, waving her hand as if they could hear her.

Zayden joined in her laughter, his deep chuckle filling the room. *"Don't worry, they'll understand. And if they don't, well, we're married now. We can face their judgment together."*

Sabrina felt a sense of comfort and ease with Zayden that she hadn't expected. As they continued talking, they discovered more similarities and shared interests. They both loved theme parks and roller coasters, and they bonded over their mutual love for Mexican food and sci-fi movies. The conversation flowed effortlessly, and they found themselves laughing and teasing each other like old friends.

"I have a question for you?" Zayden asked.

"Sure."

"Our kiss, what did you think about it?"

Heat rushed through Sabrina's body as her eyes opened wide.

"It was good. I'm not going to lie."

"Yeah, I like it too. I still get goosebumps thinking of it."

"Did you want kiss me again?" She asked, giving him a sultry look.

"Can I?"

"I mean were married now, right?"

"Oh, yeah." He grinned, leaning forward to kiss her.

Just before Zayden could kiss her, the sound of their names being called interrupted their private moment. *"Zayden! Sabrina! We need you for the reception!"* It was Emma, the show's producer, her voice echoing through the hotel's hallway.

Zayden and Sabrina exchanged a quick glance, their eyes filled with disappointment at being interrupted. *"We should probably go,"* Zayden said, rising from the couch. *"We don't want to keep everyone waiting."*

Sabrina nodded, a hint of sadness in her eyes. *"Raincheck on the kiss?"*

"Yeah, definitely." Zayden smirked.

"I wish we had more time to talk. There's so much I want to know about you."

Zayden took her hand in his, his touch sending a tingle up her arm. *"We have our entire lives to talk, Sabrina. This is just the beginning. And who knows, maybe we'll discover even more secrets along the way."*

Sabrina smiled, her heart racing at the thought of uncovering more about this intriguing man she had married. As they made their way out of the secluded room, hand in hand, Sabrina was happy to call the man that held her hand her husband.

Chapter 6

As the DJ announced their names, Zayden and Sabrina Moss entered the reception venue hand in hand. The chairs had been removed, and a dance floor now took center stage, surrounded by beautifully decorated tables. The atmosphere was electric, with the buzz of conversation filling the air. This was it; there was no turning back now. Sabrina, felt her heart race as she realized she was now part of a married couple. She was now Mrs. Moss. It was a surreal feeling, and she couldn't help but wonder if this was all a dream.

During the first dance, Sabrina's nerves kicked in as she remembered her aversion to dancing in public. But Zayden, ever the reassuring presence, pulled her close and whispered softly, *"Just look at me and follow my lead. I've got you."*

And so, they danced, swaying slowly to the romantic melody filling the room. Zayden held her close, his hands gently guiding her, making her feel safe and desired all at once. Sabrina couldn't help but notice Zayden's confident demeanor, and she felt a spark of attraction as his hands softly caressed her body.

Zayden, for his part, was struggling to keep his composure. He had never felt this way before; he was usually the suave, confident one, but something about Sabrina had him completely enthralled. He couldn't take his eyes off her; the way her dress hugged her curves, accentuating her full breasts and voluptuous figure, was driving him wild. He wanted to kiss her passionately, but he held back, knowing that their first kiss as husband and wife deserved to be something special.

As the song drew to a close, they paused, their eyes locking, communicating a thousand unspoken words. And then, in a moment that felt like an electric shock to them both, Zayden leaned forward and claimed Sabrina's lips in a deep, soul-stirring kiss. It was different from their first kiss; this one was filled with raw emotion and a sense of discovery. It was a kiss that said, *"I choose you,"* and it left them both breathless.

The crowd erupted in cheers, their applause filling the room. Sabrina, her heart fluttering, felt a rush of emotions. She barely knew this man, and yet she was falling for him hard and fast. There was something about Zayden that made her want to let go of her usual reserved nature and embrace this wild adventure.

As they made their way through the reception, Zayden caught up with his former teammates from North Carolina University. He excitedly greeted them, his eyes shining with pride and affection. *"Guys, Isn't Sabrina gorgeous?"*

His teammates, a rowdy bunch, hollered and whistled their approval. *"Damn, Zay, you finally settled down! And with a bombshell like this! You lucky dog!"*

Zayden beamed, unable to contain his joy. *"I know, right? I mean, look at her. She's a nurse, too, can you believe it? And those curves... I can't get enough."*

The guys nudged each other, grinning widely. *"So, Zay, we know you've only dated sisters before. What's it like being with an Asian woman?"*

Zayden shrugged, a playful smile on his face. *"You know, I never thought I'd end up with someone so different from my usual type, but there's just something about Sabrina. It's not just her looks, though, of course, they're incredible. But it's her personality, too. She's got this sweet, shy thing going on, but I can tell there's a fierce, rebellious side to her as well. It's a whole new experience for me, and I'm loving it."*

One of his friends, a burly former offensive lineman, raised an eyebrow. *"So, you good with the whole interracial thing? You know, your family and all?"*

Zayden waved off the concern. *"Are you kidding? My family loves her already. And they're just as excited as I am to see me with someone who... well, let's just say her curves are appreciated."* He winked, his friends laughing along.

"So, man, you plannin' on sealing the deal tonight? You know, consummating the marriage?" one of his teammates asked, a mischievous glint in his eye.

Zayden hesitated, a slight blush creeping onto his cheeks. *"I mean, that's up to Sabrina. I'm not going to pressure her into anything. But let's just say, with a body like hers, I'm definitely hoping for it. I have a feeling the sex would be out of this world."*

Meanwhile, on the other side of the room, Sabrina found herself surrounded by her colleagues from the hospital. They couldn't get enough of Zayden, their eyes sparkling with curiosity and excitement.

"Oh my God, Sabrina, he's so hot! A teacher, too, how cute!"

Sabrina smiled, feeling a warm glow spread across her cheeks. *"I know, right? I can't believe he's mine. And those tattoos, that muscular body... he's like a bad boy with a heart of gold."*

Her friends giggled, nudging each other. *"And that dance you two shared... whew, we could feel the chemistry from across the room! That kiss though!"*

Sabrina felt herself blushing even more. *"I know, I can't believe I just kissed a stranger like that in front of everyone. It felt so right, though. I've never felt this way before."*

One of her coworkers, a bubbly blonde nurse, raised an eyebrow. *"So, are you gonna do it? You know... consummate the marriage on your wedding night?"*

The other nurses giggled, and Sabrina felt a rush of embarrassment. She took a sip of her drink, trying to gather her thoughts. *"I don't know... I mean, before I met him, I didn't think I would. But now... I don't know, there's something about him that makes me want to throw caution to the wind. I mean, look at him!"*

They all turned to admire Zayden, who was laughing with his friends, his body language relaxed and confident.

"Seriously, though," Sabrina continued, *"I've never felt this kind of connection with anyone before. He makes me want to explore this physical side of our relationship, even though I barely know him."*

Her friends nodded in understanding, their curiosity satisfied for the moment. They knew that Sabrina had always been a cautious person, but it seemed that Zayden had unlocked a side of her that was ready to embrace passion and adventure.

Chapter 7

As the sun began its slow descent, casting a warm glow over the wedding reception, Zayden and Sabrina found themselves seated at a table for two, a sumptuous meal laid out before them. It was their first opportunity to truly engage in uninterrupted conversation, and they seized it eagerly. The butter-soft steak and juicy lobster, the garlic mashed potatoes, green beans, and, of course, a generous pour of champagne, set the perfect stage for a relaxed and revealing dinner.

Zayden, ever the gentleman, allowed Sabrina to begin her tale, slicing into the tender steak as she spoke. She shared a glimpse into her past, painting a picture of herself as a solitary figure. *"Being an only child, I often wished for siblings to play with. My father, a busy surgeon, was often absent, and my mother, while loving, adhered to the traditional Korean household duties. I yearned for a livelier, more boisterous family dynamic like the ones I saw on TV."*

She paused, twirling her fork in the delicate lobster meat, a slight frown crossing her features. *"My father, Steven, could be quite tough. He had high expectations for me, and any deviation from his standards was met with disappointment. I always felt like I was falling short, never quite measuring up to his idea of the perfect daughter."*

Zayden nodded, understanding flashing in his eyes. *"I can relate to having a strict father. Mine was a taskmaster when it came to my grades. He'd played professional football and knew the value of a good education. I had to keep my grades up if I wanted to continue playing sports. It wasn't all bad though, I understood the importance of hard work."*

Reaching out, he placed his hand over hers, his touch warm and reassuring. *"Don't be too hard on your dad. Sometimes parents just want the best for their kids, and they don't always know the best way to show it."* Sabrina offered a small smile, squeezing his hand briefly before releasing it to take a sip of her champagne. *"I suppose so. I just wish he'd been more open to my choices, like your father. It's amazing that he went from a football star to helping intercity youths. That's so admirable."*

Zayden's face lit up as he spoke of his family. *"Yeah, well, my old man knew the value of giving back. I come from a big family—three brothers, can you believe it? We were always playing sports, getting into mischief. But we stuck together, and our parents made sure we stayed connected. Thanksgiving was always a blast, with all of us gathered around the TV, cheering on our favorite teams."*

Sabrina listened, a pang of longing evident in her eyes. *"I always wanted a big family. My parents were so focused on my education that holidays often passed by without much celebration. It must be wonderful to have such a close-knit family."*

"It is," Zayden agreed, taking a hearty bite of his steak. *"And I intend to carry on those traditions. I want a big family, lots of kids running around, making memories. What about you? Do you see yourself having a large family one day?"*

Sabrina blushed, lowering her eyes as she toyed with her champagne flute. *"I do. I've always dreamed of having three children. It might sound silly, but I want them to have the siblings I never had. I want them to experience the joy of a loud, loving household."*

Zayden's grin was infectious, his white teeth flashing in the soft lighting. *"Three, huh? Well, that's a challenge I accept. Let's make it happen."*

Their connection deepened as they continued to share stories of their pasts, laughing and occasionally straying into more serious topics. It was as if they were the only two people in the room, oblivious to the bustling activity around them.

As their plates were cleared, a new course was served—a rich, decadent chocolate cake with fresh berries. It was a sweet finale to their meal, and a fitting metaphor for the sweetness that was growing between them.

With the dessert, they moved on to meet their respective in-laws, an experience that proved to be a rollercoaster of emotions. Zayden's parents, Shari and Jonathan, approached their table first, their faces wreathed in warm smiles. Shari, an elegant woman with a gentle spirit, embraced Sabrina, complimenting her choice of wedding dress and expressing their delight at having a nurse in the family.

Jonathan, his muscular frame filling the space beside his wife, added his agreement, his eyes twinkling. *"And she likes football, too! Zayden, my boy, you've found yourself a catch. We're so happy to welcome Sabrina into our family."*

Sabrina, overwhelmed by their instant acceptance, felt her eyes sting with unexpected tears. She had always craved this kind of unconditional welcome, and she found herself blurting out her thanks, her voice thick with emotion.

Zayden, sensing her reaction, squeezed her hand under the table, offering silent support.

The couple then turned to greet Sabrina's parents, Steven and Debra. The Chuns, however, did not mirror the Mosses' warm welcome. As they drew near, their faces were impassive, their bodies stiff. Steven, his mouth set in a thin line, offered a curt nod, his eyes narrowing as he took in Zayden's appearance.

Debra, her long hair sleek and glossy, managed a tight smile, but it did not reach her eyes. *"We did not expect this, Sabrina,"* she said, her voice low and sharp. *"Marrying a black man was not what we envisioned for you. You could have married someone from our community, someone who shares our culture and values."*

Steven's gaze flickered to the cameras, a flash of anger crossing his features before he schooled his expression into indifference. *"This was a mistake, Sabrina. A grave mistake."*

Sabrina, her face drained of color, struggled to find her voice. She opened her mouth to speak, but no words came out. The rejection stung, cutting deep into her heart.

Zayden, sensing her distress, stood and placed a protective arm around her. *"Sabrina is my wife now, and I will care for her and love her as long as I live. I'm sorry you feel this way, but I hope that we can all move forward and make the best of this situation."*

His words were met with silence. Steven and Debra turned away, their disappointed glances stabbing at Sabrina like daggers. The hurt in Sabrina's eyes transformed into determination, and with a small smile, she leaned into Zayden, grateful for his unwavering support.

Holding her chin gently, he brushed his lips softly against hers, a tender gesture that spoke volumes. In that kiss, Sabrina found the comfort and assurance she needed, a promise that Zayden would stand by her side no matter what challenges lay ahead.

As the evening drew to a close, the newlyweds, now buoyed by the support they had found in each other, exited the reception hand in hand. Their future was uncertain, but together, they would face whatever lay ahead, embracing the adventure that life had unexpectedly thrown their way.

Chapter 8

As the reception drew to a close, Zayden and Sabrina made their way upstairs to the honeymoon suite. The moment they stepped into the room, they were greeted by a captivating sight. The soft glow of candlelight filled the room, illuminating the bed of roses that adorned the king-sized bed. Champagne bubbles glistened in two flutes, and a bowl of chocolate-covered strawberries added a touch of indulgent sweetness to the scene. The gentle moonlight shining through the floor-to-ceiling windows provided a breathtaking backdrop, reflecting off the dark waters of the ocean outside.

Zayden took Sabrina's hand and led her towards the center of the room, where they slowly danced to the soft melody playing in the background. She felt herself relax in his strong embrace, her head resting on his broad chest. It had been an emotionally charged day, and she was grateful for his unwavering support.

"Thank you for being there for me," she whispered softly, looking up at him.

Zayden smiled, his eyes shining with warmth and affection. *"Anytime, Mrs. Moss. You're my wife now, and I'll always have your back."*

Their lips met in a passionate kiss, sealing their promise to always be there for each other. The kiss deepened, their tongues tangling together as they explored each other's mouths. It was a kiss filled with promise—a promise of the endless possibilities that lay ahead for them. As they parted, breathless, Zayden asked gently, *"Are you ready for bed, Mrs. Moss?"*

Sabrina nodded, her heart fluttering with anticipation. Little did she know that their private moment was about to become even more intimate.

The camera operator, Emma, chose that moment to turn off her camera, signaling the end of their recording for the day. *I think we've got everything we need for now. You two have a good night,"* she said with a wink, as if she knew something they didn't.

The presence of cameras had become a constant in their lives, and the sudden absence of it now felt oddly liberating. Zayden and Sabrina suddenly found themselves free to be themselves without the watchful eye of millions of viewers.

*"So, how do you want to do this?"*Zayden asked, a playful grin spreading across his face. *"I can sleep on the couch if you want the bed to yourself."*

Sabrina raised an eyebrow, a glint of mischief in her eyes. *"Are you serious? I thought we were man and wife now. I'm not letting you sleep on the couch, Zayden Moss."*

He took a step closer, his voice lowering to a husky murmur. *"I just don't want to rush you into anything you're not ready for."*

Sabrina placed her hand on his chest, feeling the steady beat of his heart beneath her palm. *"I want everything, Zayden. I want you. When I first signed up for the show, I wasn't sure if I wanted to sleep with a stranger on the first night. But after seeing how you stood up for me with my family, after feeling this connection between us... I know I want this. I want you."*

The desire in her eyes was undeniable, and Zayden found himself unable to resist her any longer. He pulled her close, his lips hovering just above hers. *"If you need to ask if I want you, then you haven't been paying attention, Mrs. Moss,"* he growled playfully before capturing her lips in a searing kiss.

Sabrina's heart raced as she felt his desire matching her own. She pulled away, a playful smile on her lips. *"Wait for me on the bed,"* she whispered, her eyes sparking with excitement.

Zayden watched, transfixed, as Sabrina disappeared into the bathroom, his heart pounding with anticipation. He quickly cleared the rose petals off the bed, his mind racing with anticipation. He couldn't wait any longer; he wanted to feel every inch of her soft skin against his. He stripped down to his underwear, his erection straining against the fabric as he thought about being nestled between her thighs.

Moments later, Sabrina emerged from the bathroom, and Zayden's breath caught in his throat. She looked absolutely stunning in a sexy white corset that accentuated her voluptuous curves, paired with a matching white thong, stockings, and a garter belt. The lingerie hugged her body in all the right places, leaving little to the imagination.

Zayden couldn't take his eyes off her. *"Damn, you are so beautiful,"* he whispered hoarsely, his eyes roaming over her body.

Sabrina blushed at the sheer desire in his eyes, a warmth spreading through her. She bit her lower lip, feeling more desired than ever before. *"Come here, husband,"* she said, her voice laced with longing.

Zayden needed no further invitation. He closed the distance between them, his lips crushing against hers with urgency. He lifted her up, carrying her to the bed and laying her down gently among the scattered rose petals. The scent of roses filled the air as they came together, their bodies pressed against each other, their lips never parting.

Their hands roamed eagerly, exploring and claiming each other with a passion that could no longer be denied. Zayden's hands moved down to the curve of Sabrina's hips, his fingers hooking into the sides of her thong. With a swift motion, he ripped the delicate fabric, baring her to him. She gasped at the sudden exposure, her cheeks flushing with desire.

His mouth traveled down her neck, leaving a trail of hot, open-mouthed kisses along her silky skin. He reached the valley between her breasts, his tongue darting out to taste the smooth, delicate skin. His hands cupped her full breasts, his thumbs teasing her taut nipples through the sheer fabric of her corset.

Sabrina moaned, arching her back to offer herself to him. She wanted to feel his mouth on her, to brand her as his own. Zayden obliged, tugging at the laces of her corset until it loosened, revealing her creamy skin inch by inch. He suckled one taut peak while his hand teased the other, rolling and pinching it gently until she was squirming beneath him.

She reached down, her fingers curling around his straining erection through his underwear. She stroked him slowly, enjoying the feel of his length and the way he twitched in her hand. With a swift motion, she tugged his underwear off, freeing his thick, hardened cock.

Zayden growled at the loss of restraint, his hips bucking slightly as she wrapped her hand around him. He nibbled his way down her stomach, his breath hot against her sensitive skin. He teasingly nuzzled her navel before kissing his way back up, pausing to lavish attention on the piercing in her belly button that she'd gotten in college.

"You have no idea how sexy that is," he groaned, his mouth hovering above hers.

Sabrina smiled, her fingers twisting in his hair. *"Then I guess you'll have to show me,"* she challenged, her eyes sparkling with mischief.

Zayden's answer was a sultry kiss that stole her breath away. His lips trailed down her body, leaving a path of fire in their wake. He nuzzled the delicate lace of her garter belt before kissing the inside of her thigh, his breath teasing her dampening core.

With gentle fingers, he spread her folds, exposing her glistening center to his gaze. He paused, taking in the sight of her, before dipping his head to taste her. His tongue swirled around her clit, lapping at her essence as she arched off the bed with a moan. He suckled and licked, his fingers plunging into her heat, stretching and filling her as he stroked that magic spot inside her.

Sabrina cried out, her hands gripping the sheets as pleasure coiled tightly within her. *"Zayden, please... I need you inside me,"* she panted, her hips bucking against his face.

He obliged, sliding up her body and positioning himself at her entrance. With one smooth thrust, he filled her, his length buried to the hilt. Sabrina's eyes widened at the sensation of being stretched and filled by him.

Zayden stilled, giving her a moment to adjust to his size. He peppered kisses along her neck, whispering words of encouragement. *"You feel so damn good, baby. So tight and wet. Let me move, Sabrina. Let me make you feel even better."*

She nodded, her body relaxing around him as she whimpered softly. Zayden began to move, his hips snapping as he set a slow, torturous pace. He withdrew almost entirely before thrusting back into her, again and again, claiming her as his own.

Sabrina met his thrusts, her hips rising to meet each powerful stroke. She wrapped her legs around his waist, drawing him deeper still as she found a rhythm that had sparks of pleasure exploding behind her closed eyelids.

The sound of their passionate coupling filled the room—the slick sound of their bodies joining, mixed with their moans and gasps for breath. Zayden's thrusts grew more urgent, his grip on her hips tight as he pounded into her.

"Fuck, Sabrina, you feel so good. I can't hold on," he growled, his voice strained with the effort of holding back.

"Then don't," she panted, her nails digging into his shoulders. *"Come for me, Zayden. Let me feel it."*

Her words sent him over the edge. With a powerful thrust, he buried himself deep within her, his cock pulsing as he spilled himself inside her. Sabrina followed, her walls clenching around him as she cried out his name, her release washing over her in wave after wave of ecstasy.

They lay entangled, their hearts pounding and their breath coming in ragged gasps. Zayden gently disentangled himself, pulling her close so that her head rested on his chest. He kissed the top of her head, a sense of contentment washing over him.

"Marrying a stranger was the best decision I ever made," he murmured, tightening his hold on her slightly.

Sabrina smiled, snuggling closer. *"I couldn't agree more, Mr. Moss. I'm glad I took a leap of faith and said yes to you."*

They remained wrapped in each other's arms, their hearts still beating in time, grateful for the privacy that allowed them to explore their newfound love and passion without restraint. The moonlight shone through the windows, casting a silver glow over the contented couple as they drifted off to sleep, dreaming of the future that lay ahead—a future filled with limitless possibilities and enduring love.

Chapter 9

The morning sunlight streamed through the windows of the honeymoon suite, casting a warm glow on the tangled sheets and the entwined forms of Zayden and Sabrina. She woke slowly, feeling a pleasant soreness throughout her body—a testament to the passionate night she had shared with her new husband. Zayden's naked body was draped over hers, his muscular frame spooning her curvy figure. Sabrina smiled to herself, taking a moment to admire the beauty of their contrasting skin tones before gently stirring, not wanting to wake Zayden just yet.

Her fingers traced the lines of his tattoos, a unique artwork that adorned his arms and back. She loved how his body felt against hers, strong and protective. It was still surreal to her that they had taken this leap of faith together, marrying a stranger, and now here they were, intimately bound as husband and wife.

Zayden stirred, his deep voice rumbling as he woke. *"Good morning, Mrs. Moss,"* he said, his breath warm on her neck. *"Did you sleep well?"*

Sabrina nodded, a slight blush creeping onto her cheeks as she remembered the activities of the night before. *"It was definitely a good night,"* she replied, her voice soft and sleepy. *"I can't believe we did that. I mean, we're married."*

Zayden laughed, his warm eyes crinkling at the corners as he looked at her. *"I know, it's wild. Who would've thought I'd be spending my wedding night with a beautiful woman like you?"* He kissed her shoulder gently, his beard tickling her skin.

Sabrina turned in his arms to face him, her dark hair cascading over her shoulders. She couldn't help but admire his nude body, the definition of his six-pack, and the way his tattoos seemed to accentuate his muscular form. Zayden Moss was the epitome of the bad boy she had always secretly desired.

As if sensing her appreciation, Zayden flexed his muscles playfully. *"Like what you see, Mrs. Moss?"* he teased, his deep voice sending a shiver down her spine.

Sabrina nodded, a coy smile on her face. *"Definitely. Though I must admit, I'm curious about one thing."*

"Oh yeah? And what's that?" Zayden raised an eyebrow, his expression curious.

"Well," Sabrina said, her cheeks flushing slightly, *"I was just wondering if there are any tattoos in places that I haven't seen yet."*

Zayden's eyes sparkled with mischief. *"You'll have to stick around to find out,"* he replied, leaning in for a kiss.

Their lips met, and the kiss quickly deepened, igniting a fire between them. Zayden's hands roamed over her body, his touch both gentle and passionate. Sabrina responded eagerly, her inhibitions melting away in the wake of their desire.

Eventually, they parted, breathless. Zayden got up, his naked body on full display, and headed for the bathroom. Sabrina couldn't help but admire the view, her eyes roaming over his broad shoulders and the swagger of his movements.

He emerged a few minutes later, the sexy gray sweatpants hugging his muscular thighs and a tight shirt showcasing his sculpted chest. Sabrina's heart raced as she took in the sight, her desire for him intensifying.

Sabrina wanted to pull him back into bed and continue their explorations, but her urges were abruptly halted by a knock at the door. With a slight groan, Zayden went to answer it, pulling on a robe.

Sabrina quickly threw on a T-shirt and yoga pants, feeling a mix of excitement and nervousness as she anticipated who it might be.

When Zayden opened the door, Emma Rand, the show's producer, stood there, accompanied by a camera crew. *"Good morning, you two!"* Emma exclaimed, her cheerful voice filling the room. *"Hope we're not interrupting anything."*

Sabrina smiled, feeling a bit self-conscious as the cameras recorded their every move. *"Not at all,"* she replied, gesturing for them to come in. *"We were just, um, getting ready for the day."*

Emma, entered the room, followed by the cameramen. *"Well, we wanted to capture some footage of you both after your first night as a married couple,"* she explained, setting up the shot. *"So, how was it? Did you have fun?"*

Zayden and Sabrina exchanged a smile, their eyes sparkling with shared memories of the previous night. *"Oh, it was definitely fun,"* Zayden replied, wrapping an arm around Sabrina's waist.

"So, did you..." Emma raised her eyebrows, a playful smile on her face, *"you know... consummate the marriage?"*

Sabrina felt her cheeks flame, but she nodded, a soft smile playing on her lips. *"Yes,"* she said, her voice shy but holding a note of satisfaction.

Emma laughed, a warm and infectious sound. *"Wonderful! I'm so glad to hear it. And now, for your next adventure..."* She paused for effect, creating a sense of suspense. *"You'll be heading to Aruba for your honeymoon!"*

Sabrina's eyes widened, her excitement building at the thought of exploring a new place with Zayden. *"Aruba?"* she exclaimed, unable to hide her delight. *"That sounds amazing!"*

"Yes, we thought it would be the perfect destination for you both. You will also be there with the other contestants celebrating their honeymoon," Emma continued, her enthusiasm matching Sabrina's. *"Sunny skies, beautiful beaches, and plenty of opportunities for romance."*

Zayden's expression mirrored Sabrina's, his eyes lighting up at the prospect of a tropical getaway. *"That sounds incredible,"* he said, pulling Sabrina closer. *"I can't wait to explore Aruba with my wife."*

Emma beamed at the couple, clearly pleased with their reaction. *"Excellent! We'll take care of all the arrangements, of course. Just pack your bags and get ready for a truly unforgettable experience."*

As the producer and the camera crew prepared to leave, Sabrina felt a surge of anticipation for the journey ahead. Aruba represented a new chapter in their unique love story, a chance to create lasting memories and further deepen their bond.

"We're so grateful, Emma," Zayden said, his voice sincere as he shook the producer's hand. *"This is going to be amazing."*

Emma waved away his thanks. *"Just enjoy every moment. That's what life is all about, right? Embracing new experiences and creating unforgettable memories."*

With a final goodbye, Emma and the camera crew left the honeymoon suite, leaving Zayden and Sabrina alone once more. As the door closed, they shared a look, their eyes shining with a mixture of excitement and trepidation.

"Aruba," Sabrina whispered, as if saying the word aloud would make it more real. *"I can't believe we're actually doing this. Marrying a stranger, honeymooning in paradise... it's like a dream."*

Zayden smiled, his eyes filled with warmth and affection. *"It is a dream, but it's our reality. We took a leap of faith, and now we get to explore a new world together. It's going to be incredible."*

Their arms found their way around each other, and they stood there, embraced, as if drawing strength and comfort from their shared adventure. The prospect of Aruba represented more than just a honeymoon—it symbolized their willingness to embrace the unknown, to challenge societal norms, and to create their own unique path.

Chapter 10

The Caribbean sun shone brightly as Zayden and Sabrina, a freshly minted couple, landed in Aruba for their highly anticipated honeymoon. Their eyes lit up as they stepped into their luxurious honeymoon suite, a private sanctuary overlooking the vast ocean. The suite exuded romance with its large, inviting bed, an extravagant bathroom featuring his and her sinks, and a duel glass shower—a hint of the intimate moments to come. But what truly captivated them was the private infinity pool, sparkling under the midday sun.

Sabrina, a vision of beauty with her long dark hair and curvy figure, felt the warm sun caress her skin. She breathed in the ocean breeze, a mix of salty air and tropical flowers, filling her lungs with excitement and anticipation. The suite, with its panoramic view of the ocean, offered the perfect backdrop for their erotic adventures.

In the middle of the room, a bottle of champagne sat in an ice bucket, alongside a platter of fresh, juicy fruits. Zayden, tall and muscular, moved with purpose towards it. With a pop of the cork, he filled two flutes, the sound echoing through the suite. Sabrina, seated on the edge of the bed, playfully nibbled on a slice of pineapple, shooting him a sultry glance that spoke volumes.

"What?" Zayden asked, handing her a glass, his deep voice dripping with desire.

"Nothing," she purred, her almond eyes sparkling with mischief. *"It's just... you look so damn sexy right now."*

Zayden's eyes darkened as he took in her words, his gaze burning with intensity. *"So do you, baby. Come here."* He beckoned her with a crooked finger, his voice a husky growl.

Sabrina rose gracefully, her movements fluid as she closed the distance between them. Their lips met in a passionate kiss, tasting the sweetness of the champagne and the forbidden fruit of their desire. Zayden's arms wrapped around her, pulling her close as if he couldn't bear an inch of space between them.

As they parted, breathless, Zayden smiled, his deep voice warm and sincere. *"I'm so damn happy I ended up with you, Sabrina. This whole experience has been crazy, but I wouldn't change it for the world."*

Sabrina's heart fluttered at his words. *"Me neither. I'm glad I took a chance on this show. I never would've met someone like you otherwise."* She paused, taking a sip of her champagne, her eyes sparkling with curiosity. *"I wonder how the other couples are doing. We didn't get to see anyone else's wedding, did we?"*

Zayden shook his head, his eyes drifting to the infinity pool. *"No, but I'm sure we'll find out soon enough. For now, let's just focus on us."*

Sabrina nodded, her eyes roaming over his muscular frame. She bit her lip, feeling a familiar warmth pool between her legs. *"I want to go for a swim. Care to join me?"*

Zayden's gaze darkened with desire as he took in her skimpy red bikini, which showcased her belly ring and lower back tattoo. His eyes roamed over her full breasts and round ass, highlighted by the string bikini. *"I thought you'd never ask."*

They made their way to the pool, the sun warming their skin. Zayden dived in first, the water rippling around his muscular form. Sabrina followed, her body slicing through the water like a mermaid. She swam towards him, her eyes taking in his tattooed body, the water glistening on his chiseled six-pack and bulky pecs.

They swam closer, their bodies touching, electricity crackling between them. Zayden captured her lips in a hungry kiss, his hands roaming over her wet body. Sabrina giggled, a playful sound that quickly turned into a moan as their kisses became more intense.

Zayden's hands found her hips, pulling her closer. He growled into her mouth, his voice thick with desire. *"I want you. Now."*

Sabrina's eyes flicked to the cameras, a reminder of their constant presence. A mischievous smile curved her lips. Without breaking eye contact with Zayden, she called out, *"Can we have some privacy, please?"* The cameramen, understanding the unspoken rules of the show, began to pack up their equipment. Zayden, still wrapped around Sabrina, growled again, this time at the cameramen. *"Get the fuck out."*

Sabrina giggled, as the camera crew moved with haste from their villa.

Once the cameras were gone, Zayden's hands tightened on her hips, and he lifted her out of the water. He set her down on the edge of the pool, his eyes never leaving hers. With a swift motion, he untied the strings of her bikini bottom, baring her to him.

Sabrina's breath hitched as she felt the cool air on her exposed skin. Zayden stepped back, his eyes devouring her, before closing the distance between them again. He pushed inside her with one swift thrust, causing her to gasp and dig her nails into his shoulders.

Zayden began to move, his thrusts deep and purposeful. Sabrina matched his rhythm, her hips moving in perfect sync. The sound of flesh slapping against flesh filled the air, along with their panting breaths and moans.

As their passion built, Sabrina felt the coil of desire in her belly tighten. She wanted more. With a swift move, she pushed Zayden away, her eyes challenging him. She straddled him, her eyes locked on his as she lowered herself onto his length.

Zayden's hands gripped her hips, guiding her movements. Their gazes remained locked, a silent communication passing between them. The water lapped at their bodies as they moved together, building towards a crescendo of pleasure.

With a final thrust, they peaked together, cries of pleasure echoing through the suite. Their bodies stilled as they rode out the waves of their shared orgasm, their hearts pounding in unison. Slowly, they sank into the water, their limbs entangled, chests heaving as they caught their breath.

Smiling softly, Sabrina leaned in and captured Zayden's lips in a gentle kiss, their tongues tangling lazily. *"That was amazing,"* she whispered, her eyes sparkling with love and desire.

Zayden pulled her close, his arms tight around her. *"It's just the beginning, Mrs. Moss. We have a whole honeymoon to explore each other."* His eyes sparkled with mischief, and his voice held a promise of endless erotic encounters.

Sabrina's heart pounded at the thought, a mix of excitement and nervous anticipation fluttering in her stomach. She snuggled closer to Zayden, her head resting on his strong chest. *"I can't wait,"* she murmured, her fingers tracing patterns on his chest.

As they relaxed in the pool, the sun slowly began its descent, casting a golden glow over the suite. The day's activities had stirred their hunger, and they made their way inside, leaving a trail of wet footprints on the tile floor.

In the kitchen, they discovered a fully stocked fridge and sabered a fresh bottle of champagne, using the large knife they found in the suite's kitchen. They cooked a simple meal, laughing and feeding each other bites, before moving to the bedroom, where their exploration continued under the soft glow of candlelight.

The suite's large bed became their playground as they discovered new erogenous zones, whispering sweet nothings between gasps and moans. Their bodies, glistening with sweat, moved in perfect harmony, their passion burning as brightly as the Caribbean sun.

As the night deepened, their exploration took them to the shower, the hot water cascading over their bodies as they washed away the remnants of their lovemaking. Their kisses were slow and languid, their touches intimate and adoring.

In the stillness of the night, they lay entangled in the large bed, their limbs lazily draped over each other. Sabrina's head rested on Zayden's chest, listening to the steady beat of his heart. She traced lazy patterns on his chest, her eyes heavy with contentment.

"I really like you, Zayden," she whispered, her voice thick with sleep.

He tightened his arms around her, his voice a rumble against her ear. *"I like you too, Sabrina. More than I ever thought possible."*

Their eyes met, filled with a mixture of love, desire, and the promise of a future filled with infinite possibilities. Their lips met in a gentle kiss, sealing their unspoken vow to continue on this journey of erotic discovery together.

As they drifted off to sleep, the moon shone brightly through the floor-to-ceiling windows, casting a soft glow over their entwined bodies. Tomorrow would bring new adventures, new experiences, and more passionate encounters as they continued to write their own unique love story.

Chapter 11

The air was warm and balmy as the sun set over the private outdoor bar, setting the mood for an evening of cocktails and conversation among the married couples of the reality show. Tiki torches flickered, casting a soft glow across the intimate gathering, while the gentle lapping of the pool water nearby added to the peaceful ambiance. It was the perfect setting for the group to unwind and share their experiences since their lives had been irrevocably changed by the show.

Zayden and Sabrina arrived, their presence commanding attention. Zayden, with his muscular build accentuated by his open shirt and shorts, exuded a relaxed yet captivating aura. Sabrina, on the other hand, opted for a mix of bikini top and long skirt, a unique combination that showcased her curvaceous figure and unique sense of style. Their entrance sparked whispers and curious glances, with some couples already familiar with their story and intrigued by the forbidden nature of their love.

As the night unfolded, the women and men eventually split into their respective groups, sharing tales of their newfound marriages and the unique qualities that drew them to their partners. Sabrina, feeling more comfortable with the girls, spoke fondly of Zayden, her eyes shining with adoration. She gushed about his tattoos, a trait that ignited a spark within her, and how his profession as a teacher revealed a caring and dedicated side.

Victoria, paired with Josh, expressed her satisfaction with their intellectual connection. *"He's so intelligent, and we connect over our love of fantasy books,"* she said, a dreamy look in her eye. *"I've never been with a black man before, but it's been incredible. We're already planning our next steps for his fantasy book."* The girls laughed and nodded in understanding, each happy for the couple.

Brittney, seated next to Victoria, chimed in with a playful smile. *"Oh, I know all about good sex,"* she said, her eyes sparkling with mischief. *"Billy and I... well, let's just say we have an understanding. He's rich, and he knows how to satisfy me."* She took a sip of her cocktail, a playful glint in her eye, clearly unfazed by the shallowness of her admission.

The conversation then turned to Sabrina, who blushed as the girls asked about her wedding night with Zayden. *"Oh, yes,"* she said, a hint of mischief in her voice. *"It was... special."* The girls giggled and teased her gently, their curiosity piqued by the mysterious chemistry between the unlikely couple.

However, not everyone was as fortunate as Yolanda, the only woman who hadn't yet consummated her marriage with her husband, Xavier. She confessed her dissatisfaction with Xavier's physique, wishing she had ended up with someone like Zayden. *"He's just not my type,"* she said, a hint of resentment in her voice. *"I want someone who sets my soul on fire."*

Sabrina, sensing Yolanda's unhappiness, felt a twinge of discomfort. She glanced around, hoping to find Zayden and escape the increasingly intimate conversation. Unbeknownst to her, Zayden was facing similar inquiries from the men.

Zayden, always one to speak his mind, expressed his sincere attraction to Sabrina. *"I love the way she looks at me,"* he confessed, a hint of vulnerability in his deep voice. *"Her stare turns me on instantly, and I know she wants a family as much as I do."* The guys nodded in understanding, knowing the importance of finding someone who shared their dreams and desires.

Josh, paired with Victoria, echoed similar sentiments. *"I love that we can have intelligent conversations,"* he said, his usual reserved nature softening as he spoke of his wife. *"We're already brainstorming ideas for my next book."* Billy, ever the disruptor, interjected with a smirk. *"You planning on writing all day, or are you gonna actually do something?"* Zayden, protective of his quiet friend, stepped in. *"That's uncalled for, Billy. Josh is a gentleman, and he's clearly making Victoria happy."* Josh waved off Zayden's defense, a rare smile spreading across his face. *"It's all good. Writing is just one part of it. Victoria and I are very much exploring our relationship."*

Billy, ever the braggart, rolled his eyes. *"Well, you guys talk too much. Sex with Brittney is out of this world. And let me tell you, she's got better tits than your wife, Zayden."*

Zayden's protective instincts kicked in, and he narrowed his eyes at Billy's disrespectful comment. *"Watch what you say about my wife, Billy. That's not cool."*

Billy held up his hands in mock surrender. *"Chill, bruh. Just keeping it real. Locker room talk."* Zayden's gaze darkened, and he turned his attention back to the supportive company of his friends, leaving Billy to his shallow quips.

Xavier, feeling left out as the only man who hadn't yet experienced physical intimacy with his wife, expressed his frustration. Josh, ever the wise one, reassured him. *"Our relationships are more than just physical, Xavier. With Victoria, it just happened naturally. Your time will come, brother."* Xavier nodded, grateful for Josh's encouragement.

As the night drew to a close, only Zayden, Sabrina, Xavier, and Yolanda remained. Sabrina and Xavier entertained themselves with a game of checkers, while Zayden and Yolanda conversed nearby. Yolanda, unable to contain her true feelings any longer, confessed to Zayden, *"I wish you were my husband. I've always dreamed of a man like you."*

Zayden, taken aback, was unsure how to respond. *"Yolanda, I'm flattered, but I'm very much in enamored with Sabrina. She's the one for me."* Yolanda's expression turned desperate. *"But why are you with her? Before the show, you said you preferred black women. You could be with me instead. We could be perfect together."*

Sabrina, unbeknownst to the others, had approached just in time to hear Yolanda's bold admission. Her heart sank as she processed Zayden's initial attraction to black women and Yolanda's brazen suggestion. Unseen by the others, she turned and fled, her eyes glistening with unshed tears.

Zayden, sensing something amiss, spotted Sabrina's retreating figure and immediately understood the reason for her distress. *"Sabrina, wait!"* he called out, chasing after her. Leaving the others behind, he followed her into the night, determined to reassure her of his unwavering love and commitment.

Sabrina, feeling hurt and confused, found a quiet spot away from the party. Zayden approached, his eyes filled with concern and adoration. *"Sabrina, please let me explain,"* he began, his deep voice softened by the sincerity in his eyes. *"It's true that before the show, I had a type. But that all changed when I met you. You're the one I want, the only one I see. I love you, Sabrina, and I only have eyes for you."*

Sabrina, her emotions overwhelming her, couldn't hold back her tears any longer. *"But you said you preferred black women. Am I not enough?"* Zayden's heart broke at the pain in her voice, and he pulled her close, holding her gently. *"You are more than enough, Sabrina. My past preferences don't define my present or future. I fell in love with you, and it has nothing to do with the color of your skin. You are the one I choose, every day."*

Sabrina, feeling comforted by Zayden's words, found solace in his embrace. She looked up at him, her eyes shining with residual tears. *"But what about Yolanda? She seems so sure that you want her."* Zayden shook his head, a determined expression on his face. *"Yolanda is mistaken. I have never felt that way about her, and I never will. You're the one I want, the one I married. I'm falling for you, Sabrina, and I'm prepared to spend the rest of my life showing you just how much I care about you."*

"Really?"

"With all my heart."
"Aww, Zayden..." Sabrina moaned as the newlywed couple shared a passionate kiss on the beach.

Chapter 12

The crystal-clear waters of Aruba beckoned to Zayden and Sabrina as they prepared for their jet-skiing adventure. It was a beautiful day, the sun shining brightly overhead, with a gentle breeze providing some relief from the tropical heat. Both Zayden and Sabrina were excited to explore the island from the water, their competitive spirits emerging as they discussed who would be faster and more adventurous on the jet skis.

As they arrived at the beach, the vibrant blue waters and white sandy shore created a stunning backdrop for their date. They were given a quick safety tutorial before being fitted with life jackets and handed their jet skis. Zayden, with his athletic build and competitive nature, couldn't wait to speed through the water, while Sabrina, usually the cautious and uptight nurse, surprised herself by embracing the thrill-seeking side she rarely showed.

They climbed onto their respective jet skis, the engines roaring to life, and set off across the bay. Zayden led the way, his ski cutting through the waves with ease, while Sabrina followed closely behind, her heart racing with excitement. They weaved in and out of the calm waters, speeding up when the path allowed, and soon they were laughing and whooping, their voices carrying across the ocean.

Zayden performed daring maneuvers, splashing Sabrina with his wake, while she tried her best to keep up, her cries of protest mixed with delight. They ventured further out, the deep blues and greens of the sea providing a breathtaking contrast to the brilliant sunshine. The jet skis allowed them to explore hidden coves and secluded beaches, giving them a sense of privacy and adventure.

After an exhilarating morning, they slowed their pace, cruising side by side, taking in the tranquil beauty of their surroundings. Zayden reached out, taking Sabrina's hand in his, their fingers intertwining as they enjoyed the calm after the storm of their high-speed adventure. They had never felt more alive, the warmth of the sun on their skin, the salty spray of the ocean, and the company of each other—it was a moment of pure bliss.

As they returned to the beach, their adrenaline gradually faded, leaving them with a satisfying exhaustion. They helped each other off the jet skis, their legs a little unsteady, and laughed as they realized how hungry they were. The afternoon sun cast a golden glow on the world, creating the perfect atmosphere for a romantic dinner.

They chose a seaside restaurant, a quaint, open-air affair, where the sound of the gentle waves accompanied the soft music playing in the background. As they sat down, the sun began its descent, painting the sky with hues of pink and orange. They ordered margaritas to start, a cool, refreshing treat after their active morning.

Sabrina opted for her favorite shrimp tacos, the pico de gallo adding a delicious spice, while Zayden chose steak tacos, enjoying the onions and cilantro that complemented the savory meat. They sipped their drinks, chatting comfortably, the tension from their previous disagreement seemingly forgotten.

As they ate, the conversation turned to the other couples on the show. Zayden and Sabrina shared their thoughts, analyzing the dynamics and predicting potential outcomes. They agreed that Josh and Victoria seemed genuinely into each other, their interracial romance mirroring their own in some ways.

"I really like her," Sabrina confessed. *"She's been so kind to me. It's nice to have another woman to talk to who understands the unique challenges of our situation."*

Zayden nodded, taking a bite of his taco. *"Yeah, Josh seems like a good guy, too. They seem to have a strong connection."*

Sabrina's brows furrowed as she mentioned Brittney and Billy. *"I don't know, there's something about them that rubs me the wrong way. I don't think Billy is here for the right reasons. It feels like he's just here to boost his ego or something."*

Zayden's expression turned skeptical. *"I have to agree. And Brittney... she seems more interested in her social media followers than actually finding love. Their whole arrangement feels a bit forced."*

Sabrina took a sip of her margarita, the ice clinking against the glass. *"What about Yolanda and Xavier? I feel bad for her. They haven't really clicked, have they?"*

A shadow passed over Zayden's face. *"I feel for Yolanda. She's nice, but I have a bad feeling about them as a couple. Something's not quite right there. I can't put my finger on it."*

Sabrina's gaze intensified as she broached a subject that had clearly been weighing on her mind. *"What about you and her? Do you... feel a connection with her?"*

Zayden's eyes softened as he reached for his wife's hand. *"Sabrina, I want to be completely honest with you. You know I've always been attracted to black women, and Yolanda is easy to talk to because we have a lot in common. But that doesn't change how I feel about you. You're my wife, and I made a vow before God that I take very seriously."*

Sabrina's eyes searched his, a mix of emotions flickering across her face. *"But what if...?"*

A playful smile curved Zayden's lips. *"Even if you were a pink alien, I'd still be committed to you. I believe the matchmakers put us together for a reason, and I'm not about to give up on us, especially not before we've even had a chance to really explore our relationship."*

Her expression softened, and she leaned forward, her eyes filled with hope. *"Do you think... could you see a future with me?"*

Zayden's gaze held hers, steady and sure. *"Yes. Absolutely, I can. I want this to go beyond these three months. I want to see where this journey takes us."*

Sabrina's heart swelled, and she felt a weight lift from her shoulders. She leaned across the table and kissed him tenderly. Their lips met, a soft, sweet caress, as the sun's final rays bathed them in a warm, golden light. As they embraced, the worries and uncertainties that came with being part of a reality show faded into the background. In that moment, it was just the two of them, their love, and the promise of a future that they were creating together, one adventurous step at a time.

Chapter 13

The sun shone brightly as Zayden and Sabrina prepared for their double date with Josh and Victoria. It had been a few days since the cocktail evening, and the couples were eager to spend some quality time together away from the prying eyes of the other contestants. Of course, they couldn't escape the cameras that followed their every move, but at this point, they had all become accustomed to the constant filming.

Sabrina stepped out of the hotel room, looking radiant in a light sundress that accentuated her curvy figure. Her long dark hair fell in soft waves, and her almond-shaped eyes sparkled with anticipation. Zayden couldn't help but whistle as he saw her, his broad smile revealing his approval.

"You look amazing," he said, taking her hand and giving it a gentle squeeze.

Sabrina felt her cheeks warm with a blush. *"You don't look so bad yourself, Mr. Moss. I like the way those jeans hug your legs."*

Zayden, ever the charmer, struck a playful pose, flexing his muscular arms and broad shoulders. *"All part of the service, Mrs. Moss. Now, let's go meet our friends and show them how it's done."*

The two laughed as they made their way to the beach, where they spotted Josh and Victoria waiting for them. Josh, tall and skinny with glasses, waved enthusiastically, his quiet nature apparent even from a distance. Beside him, Victoria, a skinny redhead with glasses and freckles, chatted animatedly, her hands gesturing excitedly as she spoke.

"Looks like they're deep in conversation already," Zayden remarked as they approached. *"Hope we're not interrupting anything too nerdy."*

"Hey, no judging," Sabrina teased. *"We all know you're just as nerdy when it comes to sports."*

"Hey, sports aren't nerdy," Zayden protested, his deep voice bouncing off the sandy shore.

"Hello, you two!" Victoria called out, her voice carrying over the gentle lapping of the waves. *"We were just talking about our fantasy novel. Josh here has some fantastic ideas, and I was telling him we should definitely incorporate horses."*

"Yeah, I think they'd add a great element of adventure," Josh added, his voice soft but confident.

"Well, looks like you've come to the right place," Zayden said, a twinkle in his dark eyes. *"We've got horses right here on the beach for a little ride. Unless you two chicken out, that is."*

Sabrina smiled, sensing the playful competition that was about to unfold. *"No way, we're up for it! Right, Sabrina?"*

"Absolutely!" she replied, her heart racing at the thought of the upcoming ride.

The four ventured towards the horses, the camera crew and producers keeping a respectful distance as they captured the group's excitement and banter. Josh and Victoria, it seemed, were experienced riders, and they mounted their horses with ease.

"I used to ride horses back home on the farm," Victoria explained as she gracefully settled into the saddle.

"Me too," Josh added. *"I always liked it because it reminded me of the fantasy novels I read."*

Sabrina and Zayden, on the other hand, were less graceful as they climbed onto their horses. They laughed at their own awkwardness, relaxing into the moment.

"I think this is the first time I've ridden a horse," Zayden admitted.

"Me too," Sabrina said. *"But how hard can it be, right?"*

With a nudge of their heels, the couples set off down the beach, the gentle breeze carrying their laughter and conversations. At first, they kept a leisurely pace, taking in the stunning scenery of the Caribbean island. The warm sun shone on the crystal-clear waters, and the sand shimmered in the light.

"This is amazing!" Sabrina exclaimed, her eyes sparkling with delight. *"I feel like we're in a movie!"*

"Well, we kind of are," Zayden teased, referring to the ever-present cameras. *"But even without them, this would be pretty darn perfect."*

As they rode further down the beach, the competitive spirit that bonded Zayden and Sabrina emerged. They urged their horses to pick up the pace, challenging Josh and Victoria to an impromptu race.

"Let's see what these horses can do!" Zayden called out.

"You're on!" Victoria replied, her eyes flashing with determination.

The race began, and it quickly became apparent that Josh and Victoria were the more skilled riders. Their horses effortlessly galloped ahead, leaving Zayden and Sabrina in their dust.

"Wait for us!" Sabrina cried out, urging her horse to catch up.

Zayden laughed, his deep voice carrying on the wind. *"Looks like we might need some riding lessons, babe!"*

Despite their best efforts, Zayden and Sabrina couldn't close the gap. Josh and Victoria gracefully rode side by side, their horses seemingly in sync as they left their competitors behind.

"They're good," Zayden admitted as he pulled his horse to a stop beside Sabrina's. *"I didn't know riding a horse could make someone look so cool."*

Sabrina smiled at him, her cheeks flushed from the ride. *"I guess we underestimated them. But it's all in good fun."*

The couples dismounted and led their horses back to the starting point, chatting enthusiastically about the race. Josh and Victoria shared tips on riding, their nerdy passion for fantasy novels intertwining with their newfound love for horseback riding.

"You two are natural teachers," Zayden remarked as they walked. *"I feel like I might actually stand a chance now if we ever do this again."*

"Oh, we'll do it again," Victoria said with a grin. *"Maybe next time, we'll give you a head start."*

The group laughed, their camaraderie strong and genuine. They had formed a unique bond, one that went beyond the reality show and the cameras.

As they returned the horses, the conversation turned to the other contestants and the latest gossip.

"Have you heard about Yolanda and Xavier?" Victoria asked, her eyes dancing with curiosity. *"Apparently, there's some trouble in paradise."*

"Yeah, I heard something about that," Sabrina said, a hint of concern in her voice. *"What's going on there?"*

Victoria filled them in on the latest drama, explaining that Yolanda was having second thoughts about her marriage to Xavier. *"She's been spending a lot of time with one of the producers, confiding in him. I think she's questioning whether she made the right choice."*

Sabrina's brows furrowed. *"That's too bad. I thought they seemed so sure about each other on their wedding day."*

Zayden placed a comforting hand on Sabrina's lower back, sensing her unspoken worries. *"It's tough, making a decision like that so quickly. But we took that leap of faith, and here we are."*

Josh, who had been quiet during the ride, now spoke up. *"It's not easy finding the right person. That's why I joined the show in the first place. I thought it might be my best shot at finding a wife who gets my nerdy interests."*

"And it looks like it's working out for you," Zayden said, giving Josh a friendly slap on the back.

Victoria smiled softly at Josh, her affection for him evident. *"I know I joined the show for similar reasons. I wanted to find someone who could match my intellect, and I think I might've found him."*

The group fell into a comfortable silence as they walked, each couple reflecting on their own unique journey. The sun dipped lower in the sky, casting a golden glow over the beach, as if nature itself were celebrating their connections.

As they reached the end of the beach, the couples decided to continue their evening with a dinner at a local sushi restaurant. Over plates of fresh sushi and fruity cocktails, the conversation flowed easily. They spoke about their shared love for sci-fi and fantasy, their favorite books and movies, and their dreams for the future.

"You know, I'm really glad we did this," Zayden said, raising his cocktail glass in a mock toast. *"I feel like we've made some proper friends here."*

"Definitely," Victoria agreed. *"It's nice to connect with people who get you, especially in this crazy reality show world."*

Sabrina smiled, feeling a warmth in her heart. *"I know we'll definitely be hanging out more when we're all back in Virginia Beach. We should totally plan a double date again soon."*

"Or a triple date," Josh suggested, surprising them all with his sudden outburst. *"We should get Brittney and Billy to come along too. I think they'd get along with all of us."*

The group laughed, entertained by the usually quiet Josh's enthusiasm.

As the dinner drew to a close, the couples exchanged hugs, their bond strengthened by their shared experiences. Victoria and Josh invited Zayden and Sabrina to join them for a walk on the beach the next day, eager to continue their newfound friendship.

"It's been a blast," Zayden said as they parted ways. *"Let's do it again soon."*

Sabrina nodded, her heart full. *"Definitely. And we'll have to work on our horseback riding skills before the next race!"*

As they returned to their suite, Sabrina found herself reflecting on the evening and the unique dynamics of their group.

"I really like them," she said, snuggling into Zayden's side as they sat on the couch. *"It feels like we've found kindred spirits."*

"For sure," Zayden agreed, his arm wrapped tightly around her. *"It's a weird situation we're all in, marrying a stranger on a reality show. But sometimes, it seems, you can find some pretty amazing people."*

Sabrina sighed, a sense of contentment washing over her. *"It's a crazy ride, isn't it?"*

"The craziest," Zayden whispered, leaning in to capture her lips with his. And as the cameras continued to roll, capturing their every move, Zayden and Sabrina embraced the unknown future, their bond stronger than ever, ready to face whatever challenges and adventures lay ahead. Their story, full of forbidden love and unexpected connections, was far from over.

Chapter 14

The sun had set on the final night of their honeymoon in Aruba, casting a golden glow over the island. The air was heavy with the scent of salt and sun-warmed skin as the eight newlyweds gathered for drinks at the resort bar. Among them were Zayden and Sabrina, their passion for each other still burning bright.

As the drinks flowed, the conversation turned to the highs and lows of their time on the island. Victoria and Sabrina, now close friends, confided in Brittney about Billy's unfaithfulness. They revealed how Billy had cheated on Brittney with a stripper, an encounter that had been kept hidden from her. Brittney's face fell, her model-like features twisting with hurt and anger. She turned to Billy, her eyes flashing with hurt and anger.

"Is this true, Billy? Did you cheat on me?" she demanded, her voice shaking.

Billy, his handsome features hardening, tried to brush it off as a misunderstanding. *"It was nothing, Britt. Just a lapse in judgment. It doesn't mean anything."*

"Nothing? You call cheating on me with some stripper nothing?" Brittney's voice rose, attracting the attention of the other couples. *"How can I trust you now? How do I know you won't do it again?"*

Yolanda, ever the dramatic one, tried to calm Brittney, leading her away from the group as she sobbed uncontrollably. The other women exchanged concerned glances, while the men shifted uncomfortably in their seats.

Billy, his face flushed with anger and drink, glared at Josh and Zayden. *"Thanks a lot, guys. This is all your fault. You had to go blabbing your mouths, didn't you?"*

Zayden, his muscular frame tense, leaned forward. *"We did what we thought was right, Billy. You shouldn't have kept that from Brittney. She deserved to know the truth."*

"Stay out of my business," Billy snarled, his fists clenching. *"This is between me and my wife."*

Sabrina, her eyes flashing with anger, stepped forward and placed a hand on Zayden's chest. *"Don't you dare blame them, Billy. If anyone's at fault here, it's you. You should be apologizing to Brittney, not taking your anger out on us."*

Billy, drunk and furious, lunged at Sabrina, his hand raised as if to strike her. In an instant, Zayden was on his feet, grabbing Billy's wrist and twisting it behind his back. *"Touch her, and I'll break your fucking hand off,"* Zayden growled, his eyes cold. *"She's mine to protect, not yours to hurt."*

Billy struggled, but Zayden's grip was like iron. *"You think you can take me, Zayden? You're not so tough,"* he spat, his breath reeking of alcohol.

Zayden's eyes narrowed dangerously, his tattooed arms bulging as he tightened his hold. *"Try me, Billy. I'm not afraid of you. Lay a hand on Sabrina, and you'll regret it."*

Billy laughed, a hollow, drunken sound. *"Or what? You'll beat me up? You're all talk, Zayden."*

With a swift movement, Zayden released Billy, shoving him back. *"Get out of here, Billy. You're drunk and making a fool of yourself. Take your anger issues and leave. Sabrina's not interested in your toxic shit."*

Billy straightened his clothes, his face a mask of hatred. *"Fuck you, Zayden. And fuck all of you,"* he yelled at the group, storming out of the bar.

The tension in the air was palpable as everyone processed what had just happened. Sabrina, her heart pounding, felt a rush of warmth between her legs as she realized how Zayden had defended her. His fierce protectiveness ignited a desire within her that she had never felt before.

The rest of the group, shaken by the confrontation, decided to call it a night, each couple retreating to their suites. Victoria and Josh shared a concerned glance, worried about the potential fallout from Billy's outburst.

Yolanda, ever the drama queen, insisted on checking on Brittney, leaving Xavier to join the others in their goodbyes. The remaining couples hugged and wished each other well, grateful for the unique bonds they had formed during their time on the island.

As Zayden and Sabrina walked back to their suite, hand in hand, the moon cast a romantic glow over their path. Sabrina snuck a glance at Zayden, her heart fluttering as she thought about his defense of her. She felt protected and desired all at once, a heady combination that sent shivers down her spine.

"Are you okay?" Zayden asked, his deep voice rumbling with concern. *"That asshole didn't hurt you, did he?"*

Sabrina shook her head, meeting his intense gaze. *"I'm fine, thanks to you. Zayden, you have no idea how much it meant to me that you stood up for me like that."*

Zayden pulled her close, his strong arms wrapping around her. *"Of course, I did. Anyone messes with my woman, they mess with me. You're my wife, Sabrina. Nothing and no one will ever come between us."*

Sabrina felt her knees weaken at his words. *"I love how protective you are of me. It makes me feel..."* She trailed off, a flush spreading across her cheeks.

"Makes you feel what?" Zayden prompted, his eyes darkening with desire.

Sabrina took a deep breath, her hands sliding up his chest. *"It makes me feel wanted. Desired. And it turns me on like crazy."*

Zayden growled low in his throat, his eyes sparkling with mischief. *"Oh, really now? It turns you on?"*

Sabrina nodded, her lips curving into a mischievous smile. Without warning, she pulled him toward their suite, her heart pounding with anticipation.

The suite was bathed in soft lighting, creating a romantic atmosphere. Sabrina closed the door behind them, reaching for Zayden's hand. *"I want you,"* she whispered, her eyes shining with desire. *"Right now."*

Zayden, unable to resist, pulled her close, his lips crushing hers in a passionate kiss. Their tongues danced together, tasting and teasing as their hands explored each other's bodies.

With expert hands, Zayden undressed Sabrina, his fingers deftly unbuttoning her shirt and sliding down the zipper of her skirt. It pooled at her feet, and she stepped out of it, standing before him in lacy black lingerie.

"Damn, you're gorgeous," Zayden breathed, his eyes devouring her.

Sabrina's confidence soared at his words. She reached for the hem of his shirt, lifting it over his head to reveal his chiseled chest and washboard abs. His tattoos stood out against his dark skin, a beautiful contrast that never failed to excite her.

Their mouths found each other again, their kisses growing more urgent as they fell back onto the bed. Sabrina moaned into Zayden's mouth as he caressed her curves, his hands tracing patterns on her skin that left her burning with need.

With a quick movement, Zayden flipped them so that he loomed over her, his eyes smoldering with desire. *"You ready for me, wife?"* he murmured, his voice thick with want.

Sabrina nodded, her breath coming in short gasps. *"Please, Zayden. I need you."*

Zayden smiled, a wicked gleam in his eye. *"As you wish."*

He hooked his thumbs into the waistband of her lingerie, slowly pulling it down her legs. Sabrina lifted her hips to help him, her eyes never leaving his. When she was completely bare before him, a rush of desire hit her as she saw the raw hunger in his eyes.

With gentle hands, Zayden caressed her thighs, spreading them wider. His fingers teased her wetness, stroking her sensitive flesh as she squirmed beneath him.

"You're so fucking wet for me," he whispered, his eyes fixed on where their bodies joined.

Sabrina nodded, her hands gripping the bedsheets. *"Always for you, Zayden. Only you."*

Zayden groaned at her words, his eyes rolling back in pleasure as he entered her with one smooth thrust. Sabrina arched her back, crying out at the sensation of being filled by him.

Zayden began to move, his hips snapping as he set a relentless pace. Sabrina met his thrusts with her own, her nails digging into his shoulders as she matched his passion.

Their bodies moved together in perfect harmony, the slick sounds of their coupling filling the room. Zayden's eyes never left Sabrina's, his expression intense as he watched her writhe beneath him.

"You feel so good, baby," he growled, his hands gripping her hips to pull her tighter against him. *"Your pussy was made for me."*

Sabrina gasped at his words, her body tightening around him. *"It's yours, Zayden. All yours."*

Zayden quickened his pace, his breath coming in short gasps. *"I'm close, baby. So damn close."*

Sabrina tightened her legs around his waist, drawing him even deeper. *"Come for me, Zayden. Let me feel it."*

With a roar, Zayden let go, his body shaking as he filled her. Sabrina followed him over the edge, her walls clenching around him as she cried out his name.

For long moments, they remained still, their hearts pounding in their chests as they basked in the aftermath of their passion. Zayden eventually rolled to the side, pulling Sabrina with him so that she was cradled against his chest.

Sabrina snuggled into his embrace, her fingers tracing the tattoos on his arm. *"That was..."* She trailed off, searching for the right words.

"Incredible?" Zayden supplied, a lazy smile on his face.

Sabrina nodded, a satisfied smile on her own face. *"Incredible is an understatement. That was mind-blowing."*

Zayden chuckled, pressing a kiss to her hair. *"Glad you enjoyed it, Mrs. Moss. Always happy to please my wife."*

Sabrina giggled, nuzzling closer to him. *"You definitely pleased me. More than once."*

A satisfied silence fell between them, the events of the evening catching up with their tired bodies. Zayden's breathing evened out, his fingers tracing lazy patterns on Sabrina's bare back.

Sabrina, feeling relaxed and content, let her eyes drift closed. She was on the verge of sleep when Zayden's voice broke the silence.

"Hey, Mrs. Moss?"

"Hmm?" Sabrina murmured, already half-asleep.

"Marrying you was the best decision I ever made," Zayden whispered, his voice soft and sincere.."

Sabrina's heart swelled with warmth and love. She lifted her head to press a soft kiss to his lips. *"I couldn't agree more."*

With a contented sigh, she snuggled back into his arms, a smile on her face as she drifted off to sleep. Zayden held her close, his eyes reflecting the happiness in his heart as he followed her into the world of dreams.

Chapter 15

As the sun shone brightly over Virginia Beach, the happy glow that Zayden and Sabrina had acquired during their honeymoon in Aruba slowly faded as they landed back in reality. It was time to face the mundane tasks of unpacking and organizing their living situation for the next three months. The fantasy bubble of their luxurious suite had burst, and now they had to navigate the challenges of merging their lives, starting with their living spaces.

Sabrina accompanied Zayden to his house, and her curiosity about his living quarters was soon replaced with disappointment. The small ranch house, nestled in a not-so-desirable neighborhood, was in dire need of attention. The grass was overgrown, and the paint was peeling. It was clear that Zayden had not had the time or perhaps the inclination to maintain the property.

"Wow, Zayden, it's a bit... rustic," Sabrina remarked, doing her best to hide her discomfort.

"Hey, don't judge a book by its cover," Zayden said with a playful grin. *"It's not much, but it's mine. And I was thinking we could change that. Make it ours."*

Sabrina bit her lip, unsure how to respond. She had always prided herself on her neat and organized apartment, and Zayden's cluttered and unkempt home was a stark contrast.

"I try to take care of it, but teaching and coaching keep me busy. Plus, I wanted to spend my free time with you instead of cutting the grass," Zayden added, wrapping his arm around her waist and pulling her close.

Sabrina softened at his words, understanding the busy life of a teacher and coach. She couldn't help but admire his dedication to his work. *"I appreciate that, but you know I like things clean and tidy. It's important to me."*

"I know, babe, and I respect that. We can work on it together. It'll be our project. We'll make this place shine," Zayden assured her, his deep voice carrying a hint of determination.

As they entered the house, Zayden's husky, Snow, came barreling towards them, full of enthusiasm. Zayden laughed, scooping up the excited dog and giving him a big hug. *"Missed you, boy. Did you behave for Daddy's friends?"*

Sabrina smiled at Zayden's interaction with his dog. She loved animals too, and she could see how much Zayden adored his furry companion. It was another side of him that she found endearing.

"Aww, he's so cute! I can see why you missed him," she said, scratching Snow behind the ears.

Zayden put Snow down, and the dog immediately began exploring, sniffing at the suitcases and curious about the visitors.

Sabrina's eyes scanned the interior of the house, taking in the cluttered living room and the piles of mail on the counter. *"Zayden, honey, this place is a mess. How do you live like this?"*

He shrugged, a hint of embarrassment crossing his face. *"I know, I know. I didn't have time to clean up before we left. And, well, I'm not the best at keeping things organized."*

"Three bedrooms seem like a lot for one person," she commented, raising an eyebrow.

A shy grin spread across Zayden's face, and he took her hand, leading her toward the hallway. *"I got the space for my future wife and kids. I've always wanted a big family, and I was serious about finding someone to settle down with. Guess I just got a head start on the house."*

Sabrina's heart melted at his words. She smiled softly and squeezed his hand. *"I'm glad you're a planner too. I like that about you. But we need to work on your cleanliness. It's a turn-off."*

Zayden rolled his eyes playfully. *"Please, I turn you on plenty. So much so that I could have sex with you right here on these dirty clothes."* He pulled her closer, his eyes sparkling with mischief.

Sabrina laughed, pushing him away gently. *"Even I have limits, Zayden! We are not having sex on your dirty laundry!"*

Their flirtatious banter helped ease the tension that had built up between them. As they continued to explore the house, Sabrina's critical eye noticed the potential beneath the mess and disorder.

They spent the next hour collecting Zayden's belongings and loading them into the car. Snow watched with curiosity, his tail wagging as if he knew something exciting was happening.

"All right, let's head to your place, babe. I'm curious to see where you call home," Zayden said, shutting the trunk of the car.

Sabrina's apartment was located in a desirable oceanfront complex, and as they approached, the stark contrast between their living spaces became even more apparent. Her home was clean, well-maintained, and tastefully decorated.

A small, energetic Jack Russell terrier greeted them at the door, yipping excitedly as Sabrina scooped him up into her arms. *"Mama missed you too, Milo."* She covered the little dog with kisses, and Zayden couldn't help but smile at the adorable scene.

"He's so cute! I like your place, Sabrina. It's nice," Zayden said, petting Milo gently.

"Thanks," she replied, beaming with pride. *"I work hard to keep it nice. And I have a great landlord who takes care of the building."*

Zayden nodded, his expression turning thoughtful. *"It's great, but I was thinking—we could move your stuff to my place. It's bigger, and I've got the extra rooms. We can fix it up together."*

Sabrina frowned, hesitating as she set Milo down. *"I don't know, Zayden... Your place is a bit of a fixer-upper. I mean, it's sweet that you want to share your space, but I'm not sure I want to live there."*

"Hey, it's not that bad," Zayden protested, his brows furrowing. *"And at least I own it. We can make it work."*

Sabrina shook her head, her eyes flashing with determination. *"I don't want to live there, Zayden. I'm sorry, but I have standards. We can keep working on it, and maybe eventually, it'll be livable, but for now, we're staying here."*

Zayden's face fell, and he ran a hand through his hair, exasperated. *"Come on, babe, don't be like that. My dog would hate it here. He needs space to run around."*

"Then maybe you should've thought about that before signing up for the show. My place is perfect for us, and it's already clean and move-in ready," Sabrina countered, crossing her arms.

The tension between them grew thicker, and they glared at each other, both refusing to back down. It was their first real fight as a couple, and the honeymoon period seemed like a distant memory.

Sabrina turned away, heading into her bedroom to start packing a bag. She knew they had to live together for the next three months, and the thought of continuing this argument worried her. She wondered if this was a preview of their future—constant bickering and clashing over their differing lifestyles.

As she folded her clothes and placed them carefully into the suitcase, she could feel Zayden's eyes on her. The silence between them was heavy and uncomfortable.

Finally, Zayden spoke, his voice low and weary. *"Babe, I hate fighting with you. I just... I want us to be on the same page. This is our first test as a couple, and I don't want to fail."*

Hearing the defeat in his voice, Sabrina's heart softened. She turned to face him, seeing the sincere look in his eyes. *"I know, Zayden, and I'm sorry. I just have certain expectations, and I want us to be comfortable."*

He nodded, taking a step towards her. *"I understand, and I want you to be happy. We'll figure it out, okay? Maybe we can compromise. Spend some time at my place, some time here. We don't have to decide everything right now."*

Sabrina smiled, relief washing over her. *"Okay... maybe we can try that. But you have to promise to work on cleaning up your house."*

Zayden grinned, pulling her into his arms. *"I promise. And I'll prove to you that even messy guys can have their act together."*

Their kiss was passionate and tender, the spark between them reigniting after their disagreement. As they embraced, Milo and Snow came running, barking playfully as if celebrating the resolution of their owners' conflict.

Sabrina laughed, breaking away from Zayden. *"Looks like the dogs approve of our truce."*

"Definitely," Zayden agreed, reaching down to ruffle Snow's fur. *"Now, let's get your things packed up, and we can grab some dinner. I know a great burger joint nearby."*

As they continued to pack, the atmosphere lightened, and their earlier argument seemed like a distant memory. They chatted easily, making plans for the upcoming weeks and sharing ideas for improving Zayden's house.

While their living situation was not yet resolved, they were both willing to compromise and adapt for the sake of their relationship. The challenges of merging their lives were not insurmountable, and their love for each other only grew stronger as they tackled each hurdle together.

Chapter 16

The sun shone brightly over Virginia Beach as Sabrina Chun stood in her soon-to-be new apartment, feeling a mix of excitement and apprehension. It had been a whirlwind since she joined the reality show 'Will You Marry Me?', and now she was preparing to move in with Zayden Moss, the man she had fallen for on the show. However, their recent fight about where to live still lingered between them, casting a shadow over this happy moment.

Sabrina sighed as she surveyed the empty apartment, her heart heavy with uncertainty. She knew Zayden was still upset about their disagreement; he had barely spoken to her all morning. *"I'm going to go and talk to Josh and Xavier,"* he had mumbled, walking out of the apartment, leaving her alone with their dogs.

Sabrina felt like an avalanche of self-doubt was crashing down on her. She knew she was being unreasonable, but the thought of living in Zayden's run-down house made her cringe. It wasn't just the disarray and the musty smell; it represented a lifestyle that was incompatible with her own neat and organized ways. And yet, she couldn't shake the feeling that she was being an inconsiderate partner.

In an attempt to gain some perspective, Sabrina decided to reach out to the other women on the show. She called Victoria Stevens, Brittney Gamble, and at the request of the show's producers, Yolanda Green. Despite her personal dislike for Yolanda, Sabrina recognized the importance of creating compelling television, and reluctantly extended the invitation.

That evening, Sabrina hosted a cocktail party for the women, laying out a spread of drinks and snacks. As they settled in, the conversation turned to their experiences with moving in with their partners.

Brittney, her model-like looks accentuated by her brunette hair and grey eyes, began to speak. *"Things are so much better with Billy and me since our honeymoon,"* she said with a dreamy smile. *"He promised that he only has eyes for me now. The matchmakers really knew what they were doing when they put us together."*

Sabrina exchanged a knowing glance with Victoria, remembering the revelation of Billy's infidelity during their time in Aruba. *"Once a cheater, always a cheater,"* she murmured, her tone skeptical. *"I've dated men like Billy before. They can't help but stray."*

Brittney's eyes flashed with defensiveness. *"You don't know Billy like I do,"* she insisted. *"He's changed, and I'm happy. We're happy."*

Changing the subject, Victoria chimed in, her skinny frame relaxed in her seat. *"Josh and I are doing great, too. His house is amazing – it has a theater room, a writing room, and a gaming room. I've already claimed a spot for my gaming PC."*

Sabrina leaned forward, her curiosity piqued. *"So, Josh keeps his place clean, then?"*

Victoria nodded vigorously. *"Spotless. He's very organized."*

"Well, that's not the case with Zayden," Sabrina said, a note of frustration creeping into her voice. *"His house is a mess. I mean, it's disgusting. And he expects me to live there after the show."*

Brittney's perfectly shaped eyebrows raised in surprise. *"It's the woman's duty to keep up the house, Sabrina. That's probably why the matchmakers paired you with Zayden. To bring some structure into his life."*

Yolanda, her curvy figure accentuated by designer clothes, nodded in agreement. *"Zayden is such a good man, Sabrina. I'd clean up that house for him without a second thought. Don't let something petty like that come between you."*

Sabrina rolled her eyes, feeling irritated. She knew that Yolanda had a crush on Zayden, and it rankled her to hear her spouting off about how wonderful he was. *"Thanks, Yolanda,"* she said through gritted teeth. *"But I'm not sure I can just ignore my preferences. I like things clean and organized."*

Victoria, sensing Sabrina's discomfort, jumped in. *"It's up to you, Sabrina. You have to do what makes you happy. Maybe there's a compromise to be found."*

As the conversation continued, Sabrina found herself feeling worse instead of better. She smiled politely as Yolanda excitedly shared the news of her first sexual encounter with her husband, Xavier. *"It was good,"* she purred, a smug smile on her face. *"Really good. I was surprised, especially since he claimed to be a virgin. But he definitely knew what he was doing."*

The other women cheered, but Sabrina's smile felt tight and fake. She felt a twinge of jealousy hearing about Yolanda's satisfying sex life, and she couldn't help but wonder if she was being too hard on Zayden.

Chapter 17

The warm ocean breeze brushed against Zayden's skin as he stood on the rooftop terrace of the apartment complex, gazing out at the crashing waves in the distance. The sound of laughter and the crackling fire pit behind him created a comforting ambiance. Zayden took a sip from his beer, the cold liquid offering a brief respite from the lingering tensions of the past few weeks.

Josh, Xavier, and Billy joined him, a mix of drinks in their hands. *"It feels great to be back in the real world, doesn't it?"* Josh commented, his eyes sparkling with a mischievous glint. *"I mean, don't get me wrong, the honeymoon was amazing, but there's something to be said for gaming and just chilling at home."*

Billy, his rugged good looks accentuated by the fire's glow, scoffed playfully. *"Dude, how can you even think about video games when you have Victoria all to yourself? I thought you geeks were supposed to be all about the physical."* His tone held a hint of mockery, but there was a underlying jealousy in his eyes.

Josh shrugged, his skinny frame relaxing against the rooftop's edge. *"We do have plenty of sex, but there's more to a relationship than that. It's about connecting on a deeper level, and sometimes, that means sharing our love of video games."*

Billy rolled his eyes, the fire reflecting in his blue eyes. *"Well, I'm just glad to have my phone back. It's been buzzing off the hook with people wanting to know all the juicy details of the show."* He took a long gulp from his beer, a smug smile spreading across his face. *"Though, I will say, my DMs are looking a little sparse these days thanks to certain people."* He shot a pointed glance at Zayden and Josh.

Zayden, his broad shoulders tensing at the implication, rolled his eyes. *"Oh, come on, Billy. You know you brought that on yourself. You can't go around breaking hearts and expect people to cheer you on."*

Changing the subject, Zayden turned to Xavier, his expression softening. *"How are things with you and Yolanda? You two seemed to be hitting it off pretty well."*

Xavier, his large frame dwarfing the simple chair he occupied, looked down at his shoes, a faint blush creeping across his cheeks. *"We finally... you know..."* he trailed off, a shy smile spreading across his face.

The guys erupted in cheers, slapping Xavier on the back good-naturedly. Xavier, however, seemed less than enthusiastic. *"It wasn't what I expected,"* he confessed, his smile fading. *"I mean, I'm a virgin, and I wanted it to be special. But, Yolanda, she just... it wasn't great, guys."*

Xavier's expression turned somber as he continued. *"I finished early, and she wasn't exactly gentle about it. She yelled at me, made me feel like less of a man. My parents always told me that making love was something sacred, a gift from God. But Yolanda, she didn't seem to respect that."*

Billy, who had been listening with feigned interest, shook his head and stood up, downing the rest of his beer. *"Dude, you're putting way too much pressure on yourself. Sex is just sex. It's not that deep."* With that, he walked away, leaving the rest of the group in thoughtful silence.

Zayden and Josh exchanged a knowing glance, understanding the complexities of the situation all too well. *"Don't worry, Xavier,"* Zayden began, his voice steady and reassuring. *"Sex does get better with time and trust me, the more you do it, the easier it'll be to control yourself."*

Josh nodded in agreement. *"My first time was a disaster, too. It's normal to feel nervous and excited all at once. But, like Zayden said, with time and practice, you'll learn to last longer and really pleasure your partner."*

Zayden added, a mischievous smile playing at the corners of his mouth, *"And there are definitely ways to get her off without you finishing early. Foreplay and oral can be a man's best friend."*

Josh laughed, remembering his own experiences. *"Oh, absolutely. It's all about exploring and finding out what your partner likes. Communication is key."*

Xavier's face lit up with a grateful smile, his earlier embarrassment fading away. *"Thanks, guys. I just want a relationship like you two seem to have. It's clear that you truly care about your partners."* As he spoke, a wave of realization washed over Zayden. Despite their differences and the occasional squabble, what he shared with Sabrina was indeed something special.

Chapter 18

Later that night, Zayden and Sabrina found themselves alone in their shared bedroom. The tension between them had eased, and now a different kind of tension filled the air—one that simmered with desire and a hint of nervous excitement. Zayden, ever the passionate lover, wanted to make amends for their earlier disagreement. He approached Sabrina, his deep voice soft and tender, as he took her hands in his and looked into her almond eyes.

"Baby, I'm sorry," he said. *"I know I was being a jerk earlier. I just want you to be happy, and I realize now that I was being selfish. I don't care where we live, as long as I'm with you. I'll live in a box if that's what makes you comfortable."*

Sabrina's heart melted at his words. She could see the sincerity in his eyes, and it warmed her to her core. *"I'm sorry too, Zayden. I shouldn't have snapped at you. I was just... disappointed, I guess. It's not your fault."*

Zayden shook his head, his beard brushing gently against his chest. *"It's okay. I understand. I want to make it up to you. Let me show you how much I care about you."*

Sabrina bit her lip, a playful smile crossing her face. *"Oh really? And how do you plan to do that, Mr. Moss?"*

Zayden's eyes darkened with desire. *"However you want me to, Mrs. Moss. I'm yours."*

Sabrina's heart raced as she considered her response. She wanted this moment to be perfect, to reconnect with Zayden on a physical and emotional level. She knew exactly what she wanted, and her shy nature suddenly melted away. *"I want you to start by going down on me,"* she said, her voice husky and full of promise.

Zayden's eyebrows raised in surprise, but he didn't hesitate. He loved how Sabrina owned her desires and wasn't afraid to ask for what she wanted. He knelt before her, his strong hands resting on her thighs as he looked up at her with adoration. *"You've got it, baby."*

As Zayden began to kiss and caress Sabrina's inner thighs, she felt her body respond instantly. His kisses were soft and gentle, sending shivers up her spine. His hands roamed, exploring her curves, squeezing her soft flesh as he went. Sabrina closed her eyes, leaning back against the bedhead, her fingers tangling in the sheets as she savored the sensations. Zayden's kisses grew more intense, his breath hot against her sensitive skin. His beard tickled her thighs, sending delightful sensations throughout her body. Then, he gently spread her legs further apart, exposing her most intimate areas to his eager gaze. He paused for a moment, taking in the sight of her smooth, creamy skin, the subtle scent of her arousal filling his senses.

"You're so fucking beautiful," he murmured, his voice hoarse with desire. Sabrina blushed at the compliment, her cheeks pink with a mix of pleasure and embarrassment. *"Please, Zayden..."* she whispered, her voice shaking slightly.

Zayden needed no further invitation. He leaned in, his tongue darting out to taste her. He started slowly, his tongue tracing delicate patterns on her outer folds, savoring the sweet, musky flavor of her. He wanted to worship her body, to show her just how much he adored every inch of her. His hands gripped her thighs tightly, his fingers digging into her soft flesh as he held her in place.

Sabrina moaned softly, her head tipping back as she surrendered to the pleasure. Zayden's tongue teased and tantalized, exploring every crevice, lapping at her juices as they flowed freely. He sucked gently on her sensitive bud, his tongue flicking back and forth, sending waves of pleasure crashing through her. Her hips bucked involuntarily, grinding against his face as she sought more stimulation.

"Fuck, you taste so good," Zayden growled, his voice muffled against her core.

Sabrina's breath quickened as she neared the peak. *"Oh God, Zayden... I'm close... so close..."*

Encouraged by her words, Zayden increased the pressure, his tongue delving deeper, his fingers reaching up to massage her swollen clit. He wanted to feel her come apart in his mouth, to taste her release. And soon, her body obeyed, shaking and trembling as her orgasm washed over her. She cried out, her hands clutching at the bedsheets as wave after wave of pleasure ripped through her.

Zayden savored her essence, riding out her orgasm with her, his tongue lapping gently at her oversensitive flesh. Gradually, her body relaxed, and she opened her eyes, looking down at him with a mixture of love and satisfaction.

"That was... incredible," she breathed, reaching down to stroke his beard. Zayden smiled up at her, his eyes sparkling with happiness. *"Glad you enjoyed it, baby, but I ain't done with you yet."*

With that, Zayden rose to his feet, his eyes never leaving Sabrina's as he began to undress. He shrugged off his shirt, revealing his muscular chest, his tattoos standing out proudly against his dark skin. Sabrina's eyes widened at the sight, her mouth watering as she took in the definition of his pecs and the ripple of his abs.

He kicked off his pants, now standing before her in just his boxers, the outline of his erect cock visible through the thin fabric. Sabrina's heart raced as she anticipated what was to come. Zayden stepped closer, his hands reaching for the hem of her shirt, lifting it gently over her head and letting it fall to the floor. His eyes roamed appreciatively over her curves, taking in the swell of her breasts, the curve of her hips.

"You're fucking gorgeous," he whispered, his voice rough with desire.

Sabrina blushed, feeling self-conscious for a moment before remembering the pleasure he had just given her. She wanted to return the favor, to show him just how much she desired him. She reached for the waistband of his boxers, slowly pulling them down, freeing his erect cock. It sprang toward her, thick and veined, a drop of pre-cum forming at the tip.

Zayden hissed as she touched him, his hips bucking slightly at the contact. *"Fuck, you're killing me, Sabrina,"* he groaned.

Sabrina smiled, a wicked gleam in her eye. *"Oh, we're just getting started."* She took his cock in her hand, stroking him slowly, gently squeezing as she explored his length. Her thumb swiped over the tip, collecting the bead of moisture there, and he groaned, his eyes fluttering closed at the sensation. She continued to tease him, her touch light and playful, her eyes never leaving his as she watched his reactions.

"You like that, baby?" she asked, her voice low and seductive.

Zayden nodded, his breath coming in short gasps. *"Yes... fuck, yes... but I want more."*

Sabrina's confidence grew as she sensed his urgency. She released his cock, reaching behind her to grab a condom from the bedside table. She ripped open the packet with her teeth, her eyes never leaving his, before she sheathed him with the condom. Then, she guided him toward her, positioning him at her entrance.

Zayden paused, taking a moment to appreciate the sight of her, her dark hair cascading over her shoulders, her eyes hooded with desire. *"Fuck, I'm so glad your fucking mine. Are you ready for me, baby?"* he asked, his voice thick with need.

Sabrina nodded, biting her lip as she anticipated the moment. *"I'm ready. I want you inside me. Don't make me beg."*

"Never..." he grinned.

With a groan, Zayden thrust forward, filling her completely. Sabrina gasped as he stretched her, her body accommodating his size. Zayden paused, giving her a moment to adjust, his hands gripping her hips tightly. She trembled, taking deep breaths.

"You okay, baby?" he asked, his voice rough with restraint.

Sabrina nodded, her eyes fluttering open. *"I'm good... you can keep going."*

Zayden began to move once more, his hips snapping forward as he set a steady, relentless pace. Sabrina met his thrusts, her hands gripping his shoulders, her nails digging into his skin. She loved the feeling of his hard body against hers, the sound of their flesh slapping together filling the room.

Zayden's eyes closed as he surrendered to the pleasure, his head tipping back as he groaned loudly. *"Fuck, Sabrina... you feel so good..."*

His words spurred her on, and she wrapped her legs around his waist, urging him deeper. Zayden responded eagerly, his hands gripping her ass as he lifted her, changing the angle and hitting her sweet spot.

"Oh God, there... right there..." Sabrina moaned, her back arching as she chased her release.

Zayden complied, his thrusts becoming more targeted, more deliberate as he aimed to drive her over the edge. *"Come on, baby... let go... cum for me..."*

Sabrina's body tightened as the coil of pleasure inside her wound tighter and tighter. Zayden's words, the sensation of being so full, the sight of his powerful body moving above her—it was all too much, and she couldn't hold back anymore.

"Zayden... I'm..." she started, but her words turned into a cry as her orgasm crashed over her. Her body shook, her nails digging into his skin as she rode out the waves of pleasure.

Zayden felt her climax and it pushed him over the edge. *"Fuck, Sabrina..."* he groaned, his body tensing as he found his own release, his cum filling the condom.

For a moment, they stayed locked together, Zayden's body draped over hers, their breath coming in short, sharp gasps. Then, he gently lowered himself, his weight resting on his forearms as he nuzzled her neck, placing soft kisses along her sensitive skin.

"That was amazing," he whispered, his lips brushing against her skin as he spoke.

Sabrina nodded, her fingers tracing patterns on his back. *"It was..."* she agreed, her voice laced with satisfaction.

They lay together, their bodies still connected, enjoying the afterglow of their passionate lovemaking. Zayden placed gentle kisses along her shoulder, his hands running soothingly up and down her sides.

"I'm so happy that your mine, Sabrina Moss," he murmured, his voice full of emotion.

Sabrina smiled, a warmth spreading through her that had nothing to do with their recent passion. *"Me too, Zayden Moss"*

They snuggled together, their limbs tangled, and drifted off to sleep, content and happy, their earlier disagreement a distant memory. They had reaffirmed their commitment, and now, they could face any challenge together—as long as they had each other.

Chapter 19

The sun had set over Virginia Beach, casting a warm glow across the evening sky. Zayden and Sabrina snuggled up on a cozy couch in their apartment, the cameras rolling as they settled in for their interview with Emma. The topic of the day was couple intimacy, and as the conversation flowed, Zayden couldn't help but joke about their passionate newfound marriage.

"I think we're doing just fine in the intimacy department," he said, wrapping his arm around Sabrina and pulling her close. She playfully rolled her eyes, a light blush dusting her cheeks.

"Oh, you two lovebirds are definitely in the honeymoon phase," Emma chimed in with a laugh. *"But remember, the whole point of this experiment is to see if your relationship can stand the test of time. The honeymoon phase won't last forever."*

Sabrina nodded, her expression turning thoughtful. *"That's true. We know things will get harder as time goes on. We've already had our fair share of disagreements."*

"Disagreements are healthy," Emma assured them. *"It's all about how you handle them. And one of the key things to remember is the importance of physical connection. Even when you're fighting, making sure you're still intimate can help keep your relationship strong."*

"So, you're saying we should just have sex every time we argue?" Zayden teased, earning a nudge from Sabrina.

"Well, I'm not saying it wouldn't help," Emma said with a wink. *"But in all seriousness, physical intimacy is crucial. It's not just about the sex, though that's obviously a big part of it. It's about touch, about showing*

your partner affection and desire. A simple hug or a kiss can go a long way, even when you're not in the mood for anything more."

Sabrina smiled softly, remembering the many times Zayden had pulled her into an embrace, soothing her worries and reminding her of his love.

"That's so true," she said. *"Sometimes, when I'm stressed or we're arguing, all it takes is Zayden holding me for me to feel better. It's like our problems become smaller when we're connected like that."*

"Exactly," Emma said, pleased. *"And that's what will help keep your relationship strong in the long run. Love and communication are essential, of course, but physical touch is a vital part of the equation. It's like the glue that holds everything together."*

"So, what you're saying is, we should just keep having lots of sex?" Zayden asked, a mischievous glint in his eye.

Emma laughed. *"I'm not saying it won't help! But remember, intimacy is about more than just the physical act. It's about creating a deep, meaningful connection. It's about exploring each other's desires and pushing your boundaries together. And that's what will keep your relationship exciting and fulfilling, even when the honeymoon phase inevitably fades."*

"Well, we definitely don't have any problems in the bedroom department," Zayden boasted, earning a mock glare from Sabrina.

"Oh really?" Emma said, raising an eyebrow. *"Well, since we're on the topic, why don't you two take a little break from filming tonight? Go out, have a romantic dinner, and really dive deep into your sexual relationship. Create a 'bucket list' of sorts, with all the erotic experiences you want to tick off together."*

Sabrina's eyes lit up at the idea, and she felt a familiar warmth between her legs. *"That sounds amazing,"* she said, squeezing Zayden's hand. *"I think we've only just begun to explore each other, and I can't wait to discover more."*

"Alright then, it's settled," Emma said, clapping her hands. *"Tonight, you two enjoy some time alone. Indulge in each other, push your boundaries, and remember why you fell in love. And don't be afraid to get creative!"*

As the cameras cut, Zayden pulled Sabrina onto his lap, his hands roaming over her body as he kissed her neck. *"I don't know about you, but I'm feeling very inspired,"* he murmured against her skin.

"Me too," she whispered, moaning softly as his hands squeezed her ass. *"I can't wait to cross a few things off our list."*

That evening, Zayden and Sabrina dressed up for their dinner date, laughing and flirting as they prepared for their night of passion. They agreed to take Emma's advice and create a 'bucket list' of erotic experiences, pushing their boundaries and exploring their desires.

Sabrina slipped into a form-fitting red dress that hugged her curves, the fabric accentuating her full breasts and slim waist. The hem grazed her thighs, showcasing her long, toned legs. She paired it with black stilettos and a simple silver necklace, her dark hair cascading over her shoulders.

Zayden, on the other hand, opted for a sleek dark blue suit, the contrast bringing out the deep brown of his skin. The jacket emphasized his broad shoulders, and the pants hung low on his hips, showcasing his V-line and the hint of a tattoo peeking above his collar.

As they met in the living room, they couldn't keep their eyes or hands off each other. Zayden pulled Sabrina close, inhaling the scent of her hair as he nuzzled her neck.

"You look breathtaking," he murmured, his lips brushing against her ear, sending shivers down her spine.

"You don't look so bad yourself," she teased, her fingers tracing the lines of his jacket. *"I can't wait to get my hands on you later."*

They shared a steamy kiss, their tongues tangling as they tasted each other, before heading out to their private dinner. The restaurant was an intimate, candlelit affair, with soft music playing in the background and a table set for two by the window, offering a stunning view of the moonlit beach.

As they sipped on cocktails and indulged in a delicious meal, the conversation turned to their sexual bucket list. They started with the basics, writing down their favorite positions and acts, before venturing into more adventurous territory.

"I've always wanted to make love outdoors," Sabrina confessed, a flush creeping up her neck as she added it to the list. *"Somewhere risky, where we might get caught."*

Zayden's eyes darkened with desire. *"How about it, then? We could find a secluded spot on the beach and make love under the stars."*

Sabrina bit her lip, her heart racing at the thought. *"Deal. And I want to try something else, too. I've always been curious about role-playing. Maybe we could act out a fantasy, like teacher and student?"*

A slow, seductive smile spread across Zayden's face. *"I think that can be arranged. And in return, I've got a fantasy of my own. I want to tie you up, have you completely at my mercy."*

Sabrina's breath quickened at the idea, her core throbbing with need. *"Oh, I think I'd like that very much."*

As the night wore on, their list grew longer and more daring. They shared their deepest, darkest desires, pushing each other to explore their boundaries. From trying new positions to incorporating toys, and even venturing into the world of BDSM, their bucket list promised to keep their relationship exciting for a long time to come.

But they couldn't wait any longer to act on their fantasies. After dinner, they returned to their apartment, their hands clasped together, hearts pounding with anticipation.

Without a word, Zayden swept Sabrina into his arms, carrying her over the threshold. She giggled, her legs wrapping around his waist as he kicked the door shut behind them.

He lowered her to the bed, his lips seeking hers in a passionate kiss. Their tongues danced, tasting the remnants of their meal, as Zayden's hands roamed over Sabrina's body, his touch possessive and hungry.

Sabrina's dress was quickly discarded, pooled on the floor as she writhed beneath him. Zayden kissed a path down her body, his lips and tongue worshipping her soft skin. He nipped at her neck, leaving a trail of kisses along her collarbone, before paying homage to her full breasts. Sabrina arched her back, her hands threading through his hair as he suckled and bit gently, his hands kneading her soft flesh. She moaned, her head falling back as pleasure coiled tightly within her.

Zayden teased her nipples to tight buds, his mouth and teeth working magic as he paid equal attention to both breasts. Sabrina squirmed, her hands squeezing his shoulders, her thighs falling open as she yearned for more.

"You're so beautiful," he murmured against her skin, his breath hot and intoxicating. *"And you taste even better than the dessert we had."*

"Zayden, please," she begged, her voice breathy and desperate. *"I need you inside me."*

He obliged, sliding down her body and hooking her legs over his shoulders. With a devilish glint in his eye, he lowered his head, his tongue flicking out to taste her.

Sabrina gasped, her back bowing as he lapped at her core, his tongue teasing her swollen clit. He sucked and nibbled, his fingers sliding inside her, thrusting in a rhythmic dance that had her screaming his name.

Her orgasm slammed into her, waves of pleasure rocking her body as she cried out. Zayden drank her in, his name echoing in her ears as she shattered into pieces.

As her tremors subsided, Zayden rose above her, his eyes molten pools of desire. *"I love seeing you fall apart like that. But I'm not done with you yet."*

Before Sabrina could catch her breath, Zayden was inside her, his thick length stretching her, filling her to the brim. He thrust slowly at first, his eyes never leaving hers, searching for any sign of discomfort.

But Sabrina wanted more. She wrapped her legs around his waist, urging him deeper, meeting his relentless thrusts with her own hungry grind.

They moved as one, their bodies slick with sweat as they sought their release. Zayden's hands gripped Sabrina's hips, his fingers digging into her soft flesh as he pounded into her.

"Harder," she pleaded, her nails digging into his shoulders. *"I want it harder, Zayden."*

He happily obliged, slamming into her with fierce, primal need. The bed creaked in protest, the headboard banging against the wall in time with their passionate rhythm.

Their grunts and moans filled the room, a symphony of pleasure as they chased their climaxes. Zayden's eyes rolled back as he teetered on the edge, his balls drawing tight as he neared his release.

"Come for me, baby," Sabrina panted, her own orgasm building again. *"Fill me up."*

That was all it took. Zayden roared her name, his body stiffening as he emptied himself into her, his hips stuttering as he pumped his seed.

Sabrina came moments later, her inner walls milking his shaft as she cried out his name. Her body shook with the force of her release, her back arching as she rode the wave of ecstasy.

Collapsing onto the bed, they lay tangled together, their breath coming in ragged gasps. Zayden nuzzled Sabrina's neck, his hands gently stroking her skin as their hearts slowed to a steady rhythm.

"That was incredible," she whispered, her fingers tracing patterns on his back. *"But we've still got a whole list of fantasies to work through."*

Zayden chuckled, pressing a soft kiss to her shoulder. *"Don't worry, we've got all night. And tomorrow, and the next day, and the next..."*

Sabrina smiled, snuggling closer as her eyes drifted closed. *"I can't wait."*

Chapter 20

The clock struck noon, and Zayden Moss looked up from the football practice footage he was reviewing with his students. His eyes lit up as he saw his wife, Sabrina, walk into the classroom. Her curvy figure filled out her hospital scrubs enticingly, and her long dark hair fell loosely around her shoulders. A playful grin spread across his face as he took in her beauty.

"Well, well, well... Coach Moss, is this your wife?" one of the football players, Lamar, piped up, his eyes widening at the sight of Sabrina. *"She's fine as hell, coach!"*

Zayden's chest puffed up with pride as he playfully tossed a paper ball at Lamar. *"Get out of here, you dog! But yes, gentlemen, this is Mrs. Moss. Show some respect."*

The students laughed and bid their farewells, their eyes lingering on Sabrina as they left. She felt a tingle run through her body under their gaze, and she couldn't help but feel flattered by their attention.

"Sorry about that," Zayden said with a charming grin. *"They're a rowdy bunch, but they mean well."*

"It's no problem," Sabrina replied, her heart fluttering at the sight of her husband's handsome face. *"I was a nerd in high school, so it's nice to be noticed by the jocks for a change."*

Zayden stepped closer, his deep voice lowering to a husky murmur. *"I would've noticed you anywhere, baby. That ass is hard to miss."*

Sabrina playfully rolled her eyes and handed Zayden his lunch—a container of Korean BBQ, his favorite. They sat down together, stealing glances at each other between bites.

"So, how's work treating you?" Sabrina asked, curious about his day-to-day life as a teacher and football coach.

"It's good to be back," Zayden replied between mouthfuls. *"The football team has a game on Friday. You'll be there, right?"*

"Of course," Sabrina said, a smile spreading across her face. *"I wouldn't miss it."*

They ate in comfortable silence for a while, the tension building between them as their eyes met and held. Finally, Sabrina spoke up, her voice laced with curiosity. *"Isn't it weird without the cameras around? I mean, after being on the show and having our every move filmed..."*

Zayden nodded, finishing off his last bite of pork. *"Definitely strange, but it's also nice to have some privacy. How's the hospital handling your newfound fame?"*

"They're cool with it as long as I don't bring the cameras there," Sabrina replied with a shrug. *"And no criminal activities, apparently,"* she added with a laugh.

Zayden's eyes sparkled with mischief. *"Darn, there goes my plan to rob a bank with you as my partner in crime."*

"Sounds like a solid plan to me," Sabrina teased back. *"Maybe after these three months are up, we'll give it a shot."*

"Deal," Zayden said, winking at her. *"Are they okay with the more... intimate details of the show?"*

"Yeah, I mean, we're human," Sabrina said, feeling a blush creep up her cheeks. *"We're married too. What do they expect?"*

"True," Zayden agreed, his eyes roaming over her body. *"Speaking of which, you look damn sexy in those scrubs, baby. Even with all that covering you up, I can still make out those curves."*

Sabrina rolled her eyes good-naturedly. *"All you think about is sex, Zayden Moss."*

"I'm a guy, what can I say?" he laughed, his eyes glinting with desire. *"I'm always ready for action. Speaking of which, am I mistaken, or are you feeling a little turned on right now?"*

Sabrina felt her face flush even more. She knew her husband could always sense her arousal, and the thought of him knowing what she was feeling made her wetter. *"Maybe,"* she whispered, leaning in closer. *"And what if I am?"*

Zayden's lip curled into a sexy smirk. *"Well, since you mentioned it... I happen to have a fantasy about fucking you in a supply room closet, like they do in those medical shows."*

Sabrina's eyes widened, her pulse quickening at the thought. *"Those shows are full of shit, Zayden. There's no way anyone could hook up in those tiny closets without getting caught."*

Zayden's eyebrows shot up, his eyes daring her. *"Wanna bet?"*

Later that night, Zayden found himself unable to focus on anything but the memory of Sabrina's curves straining against her scrubs. Her giggle as she teased him about his constant state of arousal echoed in his mind, and he found himself getting harder by the second. He knew he had to make his fantasy a reality.

As stealthily as he could, he made his way to the hospital where Sabrina worked, his heart pounding with anticipation. He found her in one of the wards, tending to a young patient. Her back was turned to him, and he admired the way her hips swayed gently from side to side as she moved.

Silently, he approached her, his eyes burning with desire. When she turned around and saw him, her eyes widened in surprise, and a slow smile spread across her face.

"Zayden, what are you doing here?" she asked, her voice a husky whisper.

Without a word, he took her hand and pulled her toward the supply room. Her eyes sparkled with understanding, and she bit her lower lip seductively as she allowed herself to be led.

Once inside the closet, Zayden locked the door behind them. The space was small and cramped, just as Sabrina had predicted, but the limited space only added to the thrill of their forbidden encounter.

He wasted no time, pulling her towards him and crushing his lips against hers in a passionate kiss. Their tongues danced together, their hunger for each other taking over. Zayden's hands roamed down her body, gripping her hips possessively.

"I've been thinking about this ass all day," he growled, squeezing her cheeks roughly.

Sabrina moaned into his mouth, her hands reaching up to grip his shoulders. *"Zayden..."* she breathed, her voice filled with need.

With urgency, Zayden yanked down her scrub pants, baring her round ass to him. He pulled her back toward him, pressing his hardening cock against her, and reached around to stroke her wetness.

"You like it when I talk about your body, don't you, baby?" he whispered in her ear, his breath hot on her skin.

"Yes," Sabrina whimpered, pushing back against his hand. *"It makes me so wet..."*

Zayden smiled against her neck, nipping at her delicate skin with his teeth. His fingers found her clit, rubbing circles around it as he prepared to take her.

"You want my cock, baby?" he growled, his voice strained with desire.

"Yes, please..." Sabrina begged, her body on fire.

Without further hesitation, Zayden thrust into her, filling her completely. Her walls stretched to accommodate his length, and she cried out in pleasure. Zayden grabbed her hips roughly, pulling her back onto him as he began to move.

The sound of their bodies slapping together echoed in the small space, mingling with their heavy breathing and moans. Zayden's hands left bruising marks on Sabrina's skin as he fucked her with abandon.

"You feel so damn good, baby," he grunted, his hips snapping forward with each thrust. *"Your tight pussy was made for my cock."*

"Fuck me harder, Zayden," Sabrina begged, her head thrown back in ecstasy. *"I want to feel you deep inside me."*

Zayden obliged, slamming into her with force. The sensation was overwhelming, and Sabrina knew she was close to the edge. Zayden's fingers found her clit again, rubbing it furiously as he pumped into her. *"Cum for me, baby,"* he demanded, his voice rough with his own building orgasm. *"I want to feel your pussy tighten around my cock."*

Sabrina's body tensed, and she cried out as her orgasm ripped through her. Her walls clamped down on Zayden's shaft, milking him for all he was worth. Zayden growled his approval, spilling his hot cum deep inside her.

They stayed frozen in that position for a moment, catching their breath. Finally, Zayden pulled out of her, and they both straightened their clothes.

Sabrina turned to face him, her cheeks flushed and her hair mussed. She bit her lip as she looked up at him, her eyes shining with love and desire. *"I think I like your fantasy, Mr. Moss."*

Zayden's chest puffed up with pride, and he pulled her into his arms, kissing her deeply. *"And I think I like making my fantasies come true with you, Mrs. Moss."*

Chapter 21

Sabrina and Zayden were cuddled up on the couch, their arms and legs intertwined as they watched the intense football game between their rival schools. It was a rare moment of relaxation for the couple, who had just finished filming the latest season of the reality show that had brought them together. The game was a perfect excuse to unwind and forget about the pressures of their newfound fame

"I can't believe you're rooting for Virginia University," Zayden teased, nuzzling his nose against Sabrina's neck. *"It goes against everything I stand for as a loyal alumnus of North Carolina University."*

"I know, baby," Sabrina purred, turning her head to capture his lips in a slow, passionate kiss. *"If North Carolina wins, I promise to make it worth your while."*

"Oh yeah? And what exactly do you have in mind, Mrs. Moss?" Zayden asked, his eyes glinting with mischief.

Sabrina leaned closer, her hot breath tickling his ear as she whispered, *"We make a little bet. Every time Virginia scores, you take off an article of clothing. And if North Carolina scores, I'll do the same."*

Zayden's eyebrows shot up, a devilish smile spreading across his face. *"Sounds like a plan, Mrs. Moss. But let's make it even more interesting. If my team wins, you have to do whatever I want for a whole day. And if your team wins, the same goes for me."*

Sabrina bit her lip, her eyes flicking down to his broad chest, already imagining what it would feel like to have her hands all over it. *"You drive a hard bargain, Mr. Moss. But you have yourself a deal."*

And so the game commenced, with Sabrina and Zayden fully immersed in the action, their competitive natures fueling the burning desire between them. As the teams traded scores, the clothing started to come off, piece by piece.

By halftime, Sabrina was down to her lacy black bra and matching panties, her heart fluttering as she caught Zayden's appreciative gaze roaming over her body. Her cheeks flushed with a mixture of arousal and the warmth from the blanket they were sharing.

"This game is intense," Zayden murmured, his hand reaching for hers under the blanket. *"But I have a feeling the real action is about to happen right here on this couch."*

Sabrina squeezed his hand, her eyes sparkling with anticipation. *"You have no idea how turned on I am right now. I might just need to collect my prize a little early."*

The second half resumed, and the teams battled it out with relentless determination. The score remained tight, with neither side able to pull away. With each change in possession, the tension in the room escalated, mirrored by the rising heat between Sabrina and Zayden.

As the final minutes ticked away, the game remained undecided. Sabrina and Zayden were now practically glued to the screen, their bodies pressed together, the soft fabric of their underwear the only barrier between them.

And then, with a heart-stopping play, Virginia University intercepted a pass, sealing their victory in the final seconds. Sabrina let out a triumphant whoop, throwing her hands in the air, while Zayden sank back against the couch, a mix of disappointment and desire flashing across his face.

"Looks like North Carolina just couldn't pull it off," Sabrina teased, her eyes sparkling with mischief. *"I believe you have something else to take off, Mr. Moss."*

With a mock sigh, Zayden reached for the elastic waistband of his boxers, slowly sliding them down his muscular thighs. Sabrina's eyes followed his every movement, her breath quickening as she took in the sight of his powerful body, now completely bared to her.

"There," he said, his deep voice laced with playful resignation. *"I'm officially at your mercy."*

Sabrina wasted no time in taking advantage of her victory. She straddled his lap, her soft curves pressing against his hard planes. Leaning forward, she captured his lips in a hungry kiss, her hands tangling in his hair.

Zayden groaned into her mouth, his hands gripping her hips, pulling her closer. Their tongues danced together, tasting and exploring, as they lost themselves in the heated embrace.

Breaking away for air, Sabrina trailed fiery kisses along his jawline, nipping at his ear. *"You know, I could get used to seeing you like this, completely at my mercy,"* she whispered, her hot breath sending shivers down his spine.

"You haven't won yet," Zayden panted, his hands sliding up her thighs, inching dangerously close to the damp heat between her legs. *"The game might be over, but I fully intend to claim my own victory here."*

With a sultry laugh, Sabrina sat up, grinding her hips against the burgeoning hardness she felt beneath her. *"Oh really, Mr. Moss? And what exactly do you plan to do about it?"*

In response, Zayden suddenly flipped them over, so that Sabrina was now the one pinned beneath him. Her eyes widened in surprise, a delighted gasp escaping her lips as she found herself on her back, staring up at him.

"Now it's my turn," he growled, his eyes dark with desire. *"And I plan to collect on that oral favor you promised earlier."*

Without waiting for a response, Zayden kissed her deeply, his hands roaming over her body, igniting trails of fire wherever he touched. He teased her breasts, rolling her sensitive nipples between his thumbs and forefingers, causing her to arch off the couch in response.

Sabrina whimpered, her hands clutching at his broad shoulders. *"Zayden, please,"* she begged, her voice thick with need. *"I need you. Now."*

With a husky laugh, Zayden began a slow descent down her body, dropping kisses along the way. He paused when he reached her bellybutton, his tongue darting out to tease the piercing. Sabrina bucked her hips, a soft moan escaping her throat as delicious sensations shot through her.

"Zayden," she breathed, her hands fisting in the couch cushions. *"You're driving me crazy. Please, don't tease."*

"All in good time, baby," he murmured, his hot breath washing over her sensitive skin. *"I plan to savor every inch of you."*

And then, with deliberate slowness, he reached the apex of her thighs. Hooking his thumbs into the waistband of her panties, he eased them down her legs, exposing her glistening core.

Sabrina's eyes fluttered closed as she felt the cool air wash over her most intimate area, heightening her sensitivity. She could feel the heat of Zayden's gaze on her, sending shivers of anticipation through her body. *"You're so wet for me,"* he groaned, his fingers glossing over her slick folds. *"I love how much you want this."*

With that, Zayden lowered his head, his tongue tracing delicate patterns on her swollen clit. Sabrina cried out, her hips bucking off the couch as Pleasure spiraled through her. Zayden grasped her thighs, holding her in place as he continued his delectable torture.

His tongue danced and flicked, his lips sucking gently, driving her closer and closer to the edge. Sabrina's hands clutched at the couch, her body arching as she surrendered to the relentless waves of pleasure.

"Oh God, Zayden," she moaned, her voice hoarse with need. *"Don't stop. Right there. Please."*

Zayden hummed his response, sending vibrations through her sensitive core, pushing her higher and higher. Her breath came in ragged gasps as she approached the precipice, her body tingling with anticipation.

And then, with one final swipe of his skilled tongue, Sabrina tumbled over the edge. *"Zaydeeeeen!"* she cried, her body shaking uncontrollably as her orgasm washed over her.

Zayden continued his oral assault, drawing out her pleasure, milking her release until she was reduced to a quivering mess, boneless and utterly spent.

Only then did he lift his head, a satisfied smile on his face as he took in the sight of Sabrina, dazed and sated, her chest heaving as she struggled to catch her breath.

"That," she breathed, her eyes fluttering open to gaze up at him through half-lidded eyes, *"was amazing. But now it's my turn to return the favor."* She rolled them over so that Zayden was now the one sprawled out on the couch, a satisfied grin on his face. Sabrina hovered over him, her hair cascading around them like a dark curtain, creating an intimate cocoon.

Reaching for the waistband of his boxers, which were still tangled around his thighs, she slowly pulled them off, freeing his hardened length. Zayden hissed, his hips bucking slightly as he felt the cool air on his exposed skin.

"You have no idea how long I've wanted to do this," Sabrina whispered, her eyes dark with desire as she took in the sight of his thick, throbbing cock. *"I've been dreaming of having you all to myself, with no cameras or distractions."*

She leaned down, her warm breath fanning over the head of his cock, making him twitch in response. *"You have no idea how good it feels to finally make this fantasy a reality."*

Without further ado, Sabrina wrapped her lips around the tip, swirling her tongue around the sensitive ridge. Zayden groaned, his hands fisting in the couch cushions as she took more of him into her warm, wet mouth.

She set a slow, torturous pace, sucking and bobbing, her hands cupping his heavy sac. Zayden's hips bucked gently, thrusting deeper into her mouth, his breath coming in sharp gasps.

"Fuck, Sabrina," he cursed, his eyes screwed shut as he struggled for control. *"That feels so damn good. Your mouth was made for this."*

Encouraged by his words, Sabrina picked up the pace, her head bobbing faster, her lips sliding up and down his shaft. Zayden's groans filled the room, his body tensing with the effort of holding back.

"I'm close," he warned, his voice tight with anticipation. *"So damn close, baby."*

Sabrina hummed her response, sending vibrations through his sensitive flesh, pushing him closer to the edge. Zayden's hands shot out, gripping her shoulders as he pinned her in place.

"Oh fuck, here it comes," he grunted, his hips positioning up as he released his load, jet after jet of hot cum coating Sabrina's throat.

Sabrina swallowed it all, her hands gently caressing his thighs as she milked him for every last drop. Zayden slumped back against the couch, his chest heaving as he struggled to catch his breath, a look of pure bliss on his face.

"That was incredible," he whispered, reaching up to tug her down for a kiss. *"But now I want to feel you around me. I want to be buried deep inside you."*

With a sultry smile, Sabrina straddled him once more, guiding his hard length to her entrance. With a slow, torturous slide, she impaled herself on his cock, taking him all the way to the hilt.

They both groaned at the delicious sensation of being joined as one, their eyes locking as they began to move in sync. Zayden's hands gripped her hips, guiding her movements as she rose and fell, her breasts bouncing with each thrust.

"You feel so damn good," Zayden growled, his eyes fixed on the sight of their bodies joined together. *"I could fuck you like this forever."*

Sabrina moaned her agreement, her head thrown back as she savored the fullness of him inside her. She rode him with abandon, her hips moving in perfect harmony with his. Their flesh slapped together, the wet, sticky sounds filling the room as they lost themselves in the primal rhythm.

"Harder, baby," Sabrina panted, her fingers digging into his broad shoulders. *"Fuck me harder."*

Zayden obliged, his hands gripping her ass, lifting her up and slamming her back down on his cock. The couch creaked beneath them as the pace quickened, their grunts and moans filling the air.

"You're so tight," Zayden grunted, his body glistening with a fine layer of sweat. *"I'm not gonna last much longer."*

"Me neither," Sabrina gasped, her walls clenching around him as she chased her own release. *"Just a little more. Fuck me harder."*

Zayden growled, his primal side taking over as he pounded into her with relentless force. Sabrina met his thrusts with equal fervor, their bodies a tangle of feverish passion.

And then, with one final, powerful thrust, they both tumbled over the edge. Zayden roared Sabrina's name, his hips jerking as he spilled himself deep inside her. Sabrina screamed her release, her body shaking uncontrollably as her walls milked him for every last drop.

Collapsing against each other, they struggled to catch their breath, their hearts hammering against each other's chests. The room hummed with the aftermath of their passionate encounter, the air heavy with the scent of sex and satisfied smiles.

"That," Zayden whispered, kissing her softly, *"was definitely worth losing the bet."*

Sabrina giggled, snuggling closer as she nuzzled into his neck. *"I'd have to agree."*

Chapter 22

The interview with Emma was going well, or so Zayden and Sabrina thought. The couple was comfortable on the couch, their bodies relaxed and their eyes shining with a mixture of excitement and nervousness. Emma's presence was warm and inviting as she steered the conversation with her gentle questions. But things took an unexpected turn when finances became the topic of discussion.

"So, Zayden and Sabrina, we're here today to talk about a topic that many married couples struggle with: finances," Emma began, her voice gentle but firm. *"It's important to address money matters early on in a relationship to avoid future conflicts. So, I want to challenge you both to be open and honest about your financial situations."*

Sabrina spoke up first, her voice steady and confident. *"Well, I can start. I'm fortunate to have no debt. I've been diligent with my money and have a large savings account and a healthy retirement fund."* She smiled, a hint of pride in her accomplishments shining through.

Zayden shifted slightly beside her, his expression becoming more serious. *"I, unfortunately, am not in the same boat,"* he admitted. *"I don't have much in savings, and I've accumulated quite a bit of debt over the years. I live paycheck to paycheck, to be honest."*

Sabrina turned to him, her eyebrows furrowed in concern. *"Really, Zayden? How are you managing your finances, then? How are you able to afford our house?"*

Zayden cleared his throat, a hint of embarrassment creeping into his voice. *"It's a month-by-month thing, babe. I make enough to cover the basics, but it's a struggle sometimes."*

Sabrina's concern turned to determination. *"Well, if we're going to make this marriage work in the long run, we need to tackle this head-on. You need to be better with money, Zayden."*

"I know, I know," Zayden replied, his frustration evident. *"It's easier said than done, though. I'm trying to be more mindful of my spending, but it's a work in progress."*

"Maybe I can help," Sabrina offered, her tone softening as she reached for his hand. *"If you give me access to your accounts, we can create a budget together and find ways to reduce your expenses. We're in this together now."*

Zayden pulled his hand away, feeling a surge of defensiveness. *"Why do you need access to my accounts? You know I'm not great with money, but I'm not a child. I can handle my own finances."*

Sabrina's brows furrowed deeper. *"You clearly can't control your spending or create a workable budget. You're my husband now, and I won't have you drowning in debt. It affects both of us."*

Zayden crossed his arms, his frustration mounting. *"Now you care about money? You didn't seem to mind when I was paying for all those fancy dinners and trips. You never once offered to split the bill."*

Sabrina's eyes flashed with anger. *"That was before I knew the extent of your debt, Zayden. I thought you were just being generous and wanted to treat me. I had no idea you were this irresponsible with your finances."*

Zayden stood up, unable to remain seated any longer. *"Irresponsible? You're making me sound like a deadbeat. I provide for myself and I'm not asking you to bail me out. I just need some time to get my shit together."*

"Sit down, Zayden," Sabrina snapped. *"You're acting like a child. This is a serious issue, and we need to address it like adults."*

Zayden rolled his eyes and turned away, his frustration evident. *"I need a moment. I'll be right back."* He stormed off, leaving Sabrina shaking her head in disbelief.

As Zayden walked away, his mind raced. He knew Sabrina was right, but he hated feeling controlled and criticized. His financial situation was a source of embarrassment, and he felt inadequate compared to Sabrina's financial prowess.

Meanwhile, Sabrina sat on the couch, her body rigid with anger and worry. She couldn't believe how Zayden was reacting. She knew money issues could be sensitive, but she never expected him to get so defensive. She wanted to help him, but his refusal to accept her assistance only frustrated her further.

The cameras continued to roll, capturing every intense moment between the couple. Emma remained in her seat, a concerned look on her face. She knew that financial issues could make or break a marriage, and she hoped that Zayden and Sabrina would be able to work through this challenge together.

Zayden returned a few minutes later, his expression slightly calmer. *"Let's just wrap up the interview, okay? I'm not in the right headspace for this right now,"* he said, his voice strained.

Sabrina nodded, her anger softening as she saw the pain in Zayden's eyes. *"Okay, let's finish up and talk about this later. Privately."*

They refocused their attention on Emma, answering her remaining questions as calmly as they could. But the underlying tension between them was palpable, and the interview ended with a sense of relief from both parties.

As they left the studio, Zayden and Sabrina maintained a stiff silence. Zayden was seething, his anger and embarrassment bubbling just beneath the surface. Sabrina, on the other hand, was worried and confused, unsure of how to approach Zayden without triggering another argument.

During the drive home, the tension in the car was thick enough to cut with a knife. Zayden gripped the steering wheel tightly, his knuckles turning white as he struggled to control his anger. Sabrina sat in the passenger seat, silent and apprehensive, stealing glances at Zayden's clenched jaw and furrowed brow.

Finally, Zayden pulled the car over to the side of the road, the tires screeching against the asphalt. Sabrina's eyes widened in surprise, her heart pounding in her chest. *"What's wrong? Why are we stopping?"* she asked, her voice laced with concern.

Zayden killed the engine and turned to face her, his eyes dark and intense. *"I'm angry, Sabrina. Angry at myself, angry at this situation, and angry at you for making me feel like a failure,"* he said, his voice thick with emotion.

Sabrina's breath caught in her throat as she saw the raw desire burning in his eyes. She understood in that moment that his anger was fueled by something deeper, something that went beyond their financial disagreement.

Without another word, Zayden leaned in and captured her lips in a fierce kiss. Sabrina responded instantly, her body melting into his. The kiss was hungry and passionate, fueled by the raw intensity of their emotions. Zayden's hands tangled in her hair, pulling her closer as he deepened the kiss.

Sabrina moaned into his mouth, her body pressing against his. She reached for his belt, desperate to feel the heat of his skin. Zayden obliged, tearing at their clothes, needing to feel her, possess her, claim her as his own.

The car became a blur of passion and desire as they surrendered to their deepest, most primal urges. Zayden lifted Sabrina onto his lap, her legs wrapping around his waist as she ground her core against his hardening cock. He groaned, his hands gripping her ass, squeezing the soft flesh as he thrust against her.

"You drive me fucking crazy," Zayden growled, his lips trailing down her neck, nibbling and sucking at the sensitive skin. *"I hate fighting with you, but damn, it makes me want you even more."*

Sabrina giggled, a mix of delight and lust. *"I know, me too. Our make-up sex is always off the charts,"* she whispered, her hands roaming over his broad shoulders, reveling in the feel of his powerful body.

Zayden lifted her slightly, positioning her above him. *"Then let's make this the best make-up sex we've ever had,"* he challenged, his eyes burning with desire. *"Ride me, baby."*

Sabrina didn't need to be told twice. She lowered herself onto his thick length, moaning at the stretch and fullness. She began to move, slowly at first, then with increasing urgency as her desire built. Her breasts bounced with each thrust, her hard nipples brushing against Zayden's chest.

Zayden's hands gripped her hips, guiding her movements as he thrust upwards to meet her. The car filled with the sound of their passionate grunts and moans, a symphony of raw, uncontrolled desire. The leather seats creaked beneath them, the steady rhythm of their bodies creating a chaotic harmony.

Sabrina's head fell back as she neared her peak, her hands bracing against the car door for support. *"Oh god, Zayden, I'm so close,"* she panted, her body tingling with pleasure. *"Don't stop, please don't stop."*

Zayden's mouth found her neck, sucking and biting at the delicate skin as he thrust upwards with purpose. *"Cum for me, baby. Let go,"* he demanded, his voice hoarse with need.

With a loud cry, Sabrina tumbled over the edge, her body shaking as waves of pleasure ripped through her. *"Zaydeeeen!"* she screamed, her walls clenching around his cock, milking him for all he was worth.

Hearing his name on her lips sent Zayden over the edge. With a roar, he released, his hot cum filling her as he thrust wildly, their flesh slapping together. Their bodies were drenched in sweat, their hearts pounding in unison.

In the aftermath of their passionate encounter, Zayden and Sabrina lay entangled in the front seat of the car, their breathing gradually slowing. Zayden pulled Sabrina close, his arms wrapped tightly around her, seeking comfort in her warmth.

Sabrina snuggled into his embrace, her head resting on his chest, listening to the steady beat of his heart. *"I'm falling for you, Zayden,"* she whispered, her voice soft and tender. *"Even when we fight, I still want you. I still need you."*

Zayden kissed the top of her head, his hands gently stroking her back. *"I feel the same, Sabrina. I hate fighting, but sometimes it's hard to control my emotions. Especially when it comes to money. I want to be better for you."*

Sabrina lifted her head to look into his eyes, her expression soft and understanding. *"We'll work on it together. I promise. No more anger, no more hiding things from each other, okay?"*

Zayden nodded, his eyes reflecting the depth of his love for her. *"Okay. We're in this together. No more secrets."*

As they sat there, their bodies still intertwined, the sun began to set, casting a warm glow over the car. Zayden and Sabrina had just experienced another intense chapter in their ever-evolving love story, and they both knew that their journey together would be far from boring.

Chapter 23

The sunny shores of Virginia Beach set a picturesque backdrop for Zayden and Sabrina's leisurely stroll along the boardwalk. With their dogs, Milo and Snow, happily trotting by their side, the couple exuded an air of contentment and ease. Dressed casually, they presented a striking contrast: Sabrina, a vision of elegance in her yoga pants and crop top, and Zayden, embodying a relaxed charm in his grey sweatpants and t-shirt. Unfazed by the cameras trailing behind them, they focused solely on each other, their hands clasped tightly together. Their conversation flowed effortlessly as they reminisced about their unique journey so far. Zayden chuckled, recalling their initial encounters, the sparks that flew between them, and how they navigated the challenges of their reality TV romance. *"It's been quite the adventure, hasn't it?"* he remarked, a hint of wonder in his deep voice.

Sabrina smiled, her almond eyes sparkling with joy. *"Indeed, it has. And I wouldn't change a thing. Well, maybe I'd wish for a little less drama with my parents, but everything else has been incredible."*

Their fingers interlaced, a silent testament to the bond that had formed between them. *"Speaking of drama,"* Zayden began, a playful glint in his eye, *"have we ever established whose idea it was to apply for that show? I feel like it was your brilliant scheme to escape your parents' matchmaking attempts."*

Sabrina laughed, a melodious sound that drew the attention of a nearby seagull. *"It might have been! But you were the one who wanted to find someone new, tired of the usual dating scene. So, I like to think we both had our reasons for taking that leap of faith."*

Their steps brought them to a quaint bench overlooking the sparkling ocean. They sat, the warm breeze playing with Sabrina's long dark hair and the silvery chains adorning Zayden's neck. Milo and Snow plopped down at their feet, panting happily, as if they, too, enjoyed the comforts of the seaside breeze.

Zayden's expression grew serious as he turned to Sabrina, his eyes filled with an intensity that mirrored the depths of the ocean. *"I have no regrets, Sabrina, none at all. And I want you to know, if we're going to talk about our future, that I'm all in. I want us to keep building a life together, with or without the cameras."*

His words hung in the salty air, heavy with implication. Sabrina's heart fluttered as she recognized the weight of this moment. *"I feel the same, Zayden. Being with you has shown me a side of myself I never knew existed. I'm ready to keep exploring that, no matter what challenges may lie ahead."*

A beat of silence passed between them, filled only by the soothing rhythm of the waves. Then, as if on cue, Zayden and Sabrina spoke in unison, their voices layered with affection. *"So, about having children..."* Laughter erupted from both of them, breaking the tension that had begun to build. *"I take it that's a discussion we've both been meaning to have?"* Zayden teased, his eyes crinkling at the corners.

"Apparently so," Sabrina replied, her cheeks tinged with a delicate blush. *"I mean, we've talked about wanting a large family, but we've never really delved into the specifics."*

Zayden took a moment to gaze out at the shimmering horizon, as if gathering his thoughts. *"It's true, we haven't. And to be honest, the idea of being a father scares me a little. I mean, look at me, I'm barely keeping my finances together. How am I supposed to provide for a child?"*

Sabrina squeezed his hand, her thumb gently stroking the back of his hand. *"You'd be a wonderful father, Zayden. And we'd figure out the finances together. Remember, I'm a saver, and I have no debt. We can make it work, and I'm willing to support us both if needed."*

Her words seemed to ease Zayden's concerns, and a grateful smile stretched across his face. *"That's one of the things I love about you, Sabrina. You always know how to put my worries at bay."* He leaned in, his lips finding hers in a gentle kiss that spoke of comfort and devotion. As they embraced, the cameras discreetly captured the tender moment, their whispered words of love and commitment mingling with the sounds of the sea. It was a scene that would later be replayed countless times, adored by fans of their unexpected romance. But in that instant, Zayden and Sabrina existed in a bubble of their own making, unaffected by theintrusive lenses.

Pulling back, Zayden's eyes shone with a renewed fervor. *"So, we're on the same page about wanting kids, then?"*

"Definitely," Sabrina confirmed, her eyes brimming with a mix of excitement and relief. *"And you know, we haven't been using protection much. I mean, I'm not..."* She trailed off, a hint of uncertainty clouding her features.

Zayden's eyebrows shot up, his eyes widening with a mixture of surprise and anticipation. *"You're not... Are you saying there's a chance you might be...?"*

Sabrina bit her lip, a playful gleam entering her eyes as she relished the suspense she'd created. *"I'm saying that if I was..."*

Zayden didn't let her finish, pulling her close for another passionate kiss, their lips moving in perfect sync. When they parted, he gazed into her eyes, his voice steady and filled with conviction. *"I want to keep it. I want us to experience this journey together, no matter what life throws our way. And I know we're only halfway through our marriage experiment, but I'm all in, Sabrina. I'm ready to be a father to our child."*

She searched his eyes, her heart overflowing with a myriad of emotions. *"Are you sure? Because I know we said we wanted to take things slow, and we don't even know each other's families yet."*

Zayden cupped her cheek, his thumb brushing away a stray lock of hair that had fallen across her face. *"I'm sure, Sabrina. If there's one thing I'm certain of, it's that I love you and I want to build a future with you. Our families will come around, and if they don't, we'll deal with that together, too. We're a team, remember?"*

Overcome with emotion, Sabrina threw her arms around him, her face burying into the crook of his neck. *"You're right, we are,"* she murmured. *"And thank you for being so understanding about my parents. I know they can be a lot to handle, with their expectations and all."*

He held her tightly, his hands soothingly stroking her back. *"Family is important to me, too, Sabrina. And I know how much it means to you. We'll face everything as a team, and together, we'll find a way to make our families see how perfect we are for each other."*

Their embrace tightened, a tangible manifestation of the strength of their connection. It was as if the world around them faded away, leaving only the soothing embrace of the ocean breeze and the steady beat of their hearts.

Reluctantly, they parted, the warmth of their closeness lingering as they gazed into each other's eyes. *"So,"* Zayden began, a mischievous smile tugging at his lips, *"does this mean I get to start shopping for baby onesies? Because I already have an entire list of football-themed outfits picked out."*

Sabrina laughed, a joyful sound that bounced off the waves. *"Not so fast, Mr. Moss. I think we should probably take things one step at a time. But I won't deny that the thought of having a little Zayden or Sabrina running around fills me with so much joy."*

"A little Zayden or Sabrina," Zayden repeated, his eyes sparkling with delight. *"I can't decide which I'd prefer. Although, I have a feeling you're secretly hoping for a girl so you can dress her up in all the frilly, pink outfits."*

She rolled her eyes, playfully nudging him with her shoulder. *"Maybe a little bit. But don't worry, if we have a boy, I promise not to force him into tutus. Although, dancing lessons are non-negotiable. Every child should know how to dance, even if their mother dislikes dancing in public."*

Zayden feigned a shudder, causing Sabrina to laugh again. *"Fine, fine, you can teach our hypothetical son a few dance moves. But only if I get to teach him how to throw a perfect football spiral."*

"Deal," Sabrina agreed, her eyes shining with happiness. *"And who knows, maybe we'll end up with a whole team of little ones, running around and causing chaos."*

Their laughter blended with the sounds of the bustling boardwalk, creating a symphony of joy and love. Milo and Snow, sensing the shift in their guardians' moods, barked gleefully, adding to the merriment of the moment.

As the sun began its slow descent, casting a golden glow over the ocean, Zayden and Sabrina rose from the bench, their hands still entwined. They continued their walk, their steps light and carefree, as if they had shed the weight of their earlier worries.

"You know," Zayden began, a thoughtful expression on his face, *"I never imagined my life would take this turn. I signed up for that show on a whim, hoping to find someone special. But I never expected to find my soulmate, someone I could picture building a future with."*

Sabrina's heart swelled, her eyes glistening with unshed tears. *"Me neither, Zayden. I joined the show out of desperation, wanting to escape my parents' constant nagging. I never dreamed I'd find someone who understands and accepts me, flaws and all."*

"Flaws?" Zayden questioned, raising an eyebrow. *"I don't see any flaws, only perfection. And I'm not just saying that because of the cameras,"* he added with a wink.

She blushed, a warm smile softening her features. *"Thank you, Zayden. That means a lot, coming from you. You've helped me discover a part of myself I never knew existed. I feel like I can be my true self with you, without judgment."*

Their steps led them closer to the vibrant heart of Virginia Beach, where the air buzzed with the excitement of tourists and locals alike. The sun continued its descent, painting the sky in hues of pink and orange, a fitting backdrop for the love story unfolding along the boardwalk.

Zayden's voice grew softer, laced with a tenderness that mirrored the gentleness of the waves. *"You've helped me too, Sabrina. Being with you has taught me how to be more open and honest about my feelings. You've shown me that vulnerability can be a strength, not a weakness."*

Sabrina's eyes shone with a mixture of love and admiration. *"And you've shown me how to embrace life, to take risks, and to enjoy the little things. You've brought color into my world, Zayden, and I'll forever be grateful for that."*

He stopped, turning to face her, his eyes searching hers as if seeking confirmation of the depth of her words. *"And I'll forever be by your side, Sabrina, through the highs and lows, the calm and the storms. Together, we can weather anything."*

Their lips met in a kiss, a culmination of the profound connection they had forged. It was a kiss that spoke of promises, of a future intertwined, and of a love strong enough to withstand the trials that lay ahead.

The cameras, ever-present yet unobtrusive, captured the essence of their love story, a tale that would captivate audiences nationwide. But in that moment, Zayden and Sabrina were oblivious to the lenses, lost in a world of their own making, a world where their love would conquer all. And as the golden rays of the setting sun enveloped them, they strolled hand in hand, their dogs by their side, a testament to the enduring power of love, destiny, and the magical possibilities that lay ahead on their journey together.

Chapter 24

It was a sunny Saturday afternoon when Zayden and Sabrina arrived at the Moss family home for dinner. As they pulled up in their car, the cameras rolled, capturing the anticipation and excitement on their faces. The quaint four-bedroom house was a stark contrast to Zayden's usually messy and run-down place. Sabrina was pleasantly surprised to find it spotlessly clean and tastefully decorated.

Stepping inside, the aroma of grilled hamburgers and hot dogs filled the air, making their mouths water. The sound of laughter and lively conversation could be heard from the backyard, where the family had gathered for the cookout. Sabrina felt a warm glow as she realized that these wonderful people would be her family now.

In the kitchen, Shari Moss, Zayden's mother, was putting the final touches on the food. She was an older black woman with long, dark hair and an athletic build. Her eyes lit up with joy as she saw the couple enter. *"Welcome, welcome!"* she exclaimed, giving them both a warm hug. *"I'm so glad you could make it."*

Sabrina returned the hug, feeling a sense of comfort and acceptance. *"Thank you so much for having us, Mrs. Moss,"* she said with a smile. *"It smells amazing in here."*

"Please, call me Shari," Zayden's mother replied, her eyes twinkling with kindness. *"And yes, I do love to cook. I hope you're hungry!"*

As they stepped out into the backyard, the setting sun bathed the garden in a golden light. The large outdoor space was filled with the laughter of children playing games, while the adults chatted and enjoyed the food. The camera crew weaved their way through the gathering, discreetly capturing the intimate family moments.

Sabrina felt a sense of belonging as she was introduced to the extended family. Cousins, aunts, and uncles greeted her with open arms, making her feel like she had always been a part of their close-knit community. She smiled as she watched Zayden join in a lively game of catch with his younger cousins, his athletic build and broad shoulders moving gracefully as he threw the ball with ease.

"So, how was the honeymoon?" Shari asked, her eyes sparkling with curiosity as she handed Sabrina a plate of food. *"Zayden has been tight-lipped about it!"*

Sabrina blushed as she took a bite of her hamburger, savoring the juicy flavor. *"It was magical,"* she replied, a faraway look in her eyes as she remembered the passionate encounters she and Zayden had shared. *"We explored new experiences and created memories that will last a lifetime."*

Shari smiled, her kindness and openness evident in her warm expression. *"I'm so glad to hear that. And do you two have any plans for children? I know Zayden has always wanted a large family."*

Sabrina's heart warmed at the thought. *"I do want children,"* she said softly, a dreamy look in her eyes. *"I've always wanted a big family, and being a part of this one makes me realize how much I want that."* She gestured to the bustling garden, where laughter and love were in abundance. *"It's beautiful to see."*

Shari's eyes shone with happiness, and she reached out to squeeze Sabrina's hand. *"Well, I'm so happy to have you as a part of our family, Sabrina. You're a wonderful addition, and I know Zayden is lucky to have you."*

As the women chatted, their bond strengthening, Zayden found himself in deep conversation with his father, Jonathan Moss. The older man was an impressive figure, with a muscular build that belied his age. His bald head shone in the fading light, and he exuded a sense of strength and wisdom.

They sat on the patio, sipping whiskey and smoking cigars, the rich, earthy aromas hanging in the air. *"I'm proud of you, son,"* Jonathan said, his voice deep and steady. *"Marrying Sabrina was a good choice. She seems like a wonderful woman with a good head on her shoulders."*

Zayden nodded, a sense of pride and contentment washing over him. *"She is, Dad. She's supportive, caring, and has this incredible way of making me want to be a better man. I feel like I can achieve anything with her by my side."*

Jonathan smiled, his eyes wise and understanding. *"That's how it should be. But remember, being a husband is about more than just saying 'I love you'. It's about putting your wife and family first, making sacrifices, and being there for them through thick and thin. Once you truly understand that, your marriage will flourish."*

Zayden listened intently, taking his father's words to heart. He knew that Jonathan had a successful marriage and a loving family, and he wanted to emulate that in his own life. *"I understand, Dad,"* he replied, his voice filled with determination. *"I'm ready to step up and be the husband and father that they deserve."*

As the evening progressed, the family moved indoors, the women clearing the dishes and chatting in the kitchen while the men relaxed in the living room, discussing sports and current events. Sabrina found herself helping Shari and her aunts with the dishes, enjoying the easy camaraderie that had formed between them.

"You know, I've always wanted a daughter," Shari said, her eyes twinkling as she dried a plate and handed it to Sabrina to put away. *"I have four wonderful sons, but there's something special about having a daughter to share girly things with."*

Sabrina's heart melted at the warmth in Shari's voice. *"I know what you mean,"* she replied, thinking of her own strained relationship with her parents. *"My mother and I have always struggled to connect, and I've often wished for a closer bond. It's wonderful to feel that here."*

Shari smiled, her kindness and acceptance evident in her every action. *"You are family now, Sabrina. And I'm so happy to have another woman in the house to talk to and share secrets with."*

Later that night, as Sabrina and Zayden drove back to their hotel, the camera crew following discreetly behind, they couldn't help but feel a sense of contentment and belonging. Leaning her head on Zayden's shoulder, Sabrina sighed happily. *"Your family is amazing,"* she said, her eyes sparkling with affection. *"I can't wait to have a family like that of my own one day."*

Zayden smiled, his heart filled with love and gratitude. *"They accepted you so easily, just as I knew they would. And I can't wait to start our own family, too. It's going to be amazing."*

Their hands found each other, fingers intertwining as they shared a loving look. The future seemed bright and full of possibility, and they couldn't wait to continue building their life together, surrounded by the love and support of their wonderful families.

As the camera crew captured the final moments of the day, the setting sun casting a golden glow on the happy couple, it was clear that Zayden and Sabrina's journey was just beginning. Their love story, filled with passion, family, and laughter, was only just getting started.

Chapter 25

The sun shone brightly as Sabrina and Zayden made their way along the pristine Virginia Beach shoreline towards Sabrina's family home. The cameras trailed behind them, capturing every moment of their journey as they strolled hand in hand, their love and excitement palpable. Sabrina, dressed in a casual yet stylish sundress, her long dark hair flowing gently in the ocean breeze, looked relaxed and happy as she chatted with Zayden.

Zayden, tall and muscular, his skin glowing with a healthy tan, wore a casual ensemble of jeans and a button down shirt, showcasing his impressive array of tattoos. His deep voice rumbled with laughter as he shared a funny anecdote with Sabrina, their connection and chemistry evident to all who witnessed them. As they approached the extravagant oceanfront mansion that belonged to Sabrina's parents, the atmosphere became more tense and formal.

The majestic home, with its grand pillars and sweeping verandas, stood as a testament to the Chun family's success and prestige. The cameras focused on the impressive architecture, capturing the grandeur and opulence that awaited the couple inside. Sabrina's parents, Debra and Steven Chun, greeted them at the door, their faces a mixture of warmth and apprehension.

Debra, an elegant Korean American woman in her fifties, her long salt-and-pepper hair styled elegantly, offered a bright smile, her eyes shining with pride and affection for her daughter. In contrast, Steven, a distinguished-looking man with a stern gaze and salt-and-pepper hair, seemed more reserved, his arms folded across his chest in a defensive posture. The cameras captured the subtle tension in the air as the greeting unfolded.

"Zayden, it's so lovely to see you again," Debra said, her voice warm and welcoming. *"Please, come in and make yourself at home. I hope you're hungry because we have a lot of food to share."*

Zayden returned the smile, his deep voice resounding with confidence and charm. *"Thank you, Mrs. Chun. I've been looking forward to this. And please, call me Zayden. I don't stand on formalities."*

Steven nodded, his expression softening slightly. *"Welcome to our home, Zayden. We're happy to have you here. I hope you don't mind, but we're a traditional Korean family, and we like to keep things authentic."*

"Not at all, Mr. Chun," Zayden replied with a respectful tone. *"I'm excited to experience your culture and cuisine. I don't get to enjoy homemade Korean food often, so this is a real treat."*

As they entered the lavish foyer, the rich aromas of exotic spices and savory meats filled the air, teasing their taste buds. The cameras panned the spacious interior, showcasing the elegant furnishings and attention to detail that reflected the Chun family's success and refined taste.

Sabrina, sensitive to her parents' discomfort with the cameras, took Zayden's hand and gave it a gentle squeeze, offering him silent reassurance. Zayden returned the gesture with a warm smile, his eyes conveying his support and understanding. The couple exuded a sense of unity and strength as they navigated this potentially challenging family introduction.

Dinner was served in the elegant dining room, where the table was artfully set with fine china and crystal. The spread of traditional Korean dishes laid out before them was a feast for the senses, with an array of colors, textures, and flavors. Debra had prepared a multitude of savory dishes, including bulgogi, kimchi jjigae, and japchae.

As they took their seats, Steven initiated the conversation, his gaze intense as he addressed Zayden directly. *"So, Zayden, I understand you're a teacher. That's noble work, imparting knowledge to the younger generation. But I have to ask, aren't you more interested in pursuing a more lucrative career?"*

Zayden took a moment to savor a bite of bulgogi before responding, his expression thoughtful. *"It's true that I don't make much; but teaching is my passion. I find fulfillment in shaping young minds and making a difference in their lives. It's not about the money for me; it's about the impact I can have."*

Steven's eyebrow arched slightly, his skepticism evident. *"And you're content with that? With your potential, you could seek a more lucrative path. Don't you want to provide a certain standard of living for Sabrina? My daughter deserves the best."*

Zayden's eyes flickered to Sabrina, who remained silent, her eyes downcast as she fiddled with her napkin. He sat up straighter, his voice steady and sincere. *"I understand your concern, Mr. Chun. And I respect your desire to protect your daughter. But I can assure you that I'm committed to providing for her and giving her a good life. My definition of success isn't measured solely by financial gain."*

Steven's gaze intensified, his skepticism turning to borderline disapproval. *"Well, it's a competitive world out there. And with the cost of living these days, it's not easy to get by on a teacher's salary. How do you plan to support a family?"*

Zayden's jaw tightened slightly, his patience seemingly tested. *"I come from a comfortable background, Mr. Chun. I may not have the same financial aspirations as you, but that doesn't mean I can't provide for my family. I have a home, and while it may not be as grand as this beautiful mansion, it's a place I'm proud of."*

Steven's expression turned dismissive as he glanced around the opulent dining room. *"A home is an investment, Zayden. It's about providing stability and security for your family. I've heard about the shack you live in. Let's be honest, it's not suitable for raising a family."*

The tension in the room escalated, with Sabrina looking increasingly uncomfortable, her cheeks flushed. Debra, sensing the mounting friction, gently placed her hand on her husband's arm, her eyes pleading for him to ease up. Steven, however, was not deterred.

"Marrying your daughter is a significant responsibility," he continued, his tone becoming more assertive. *"And I have to be frank—I believe it was a mistake. You may be content with your career choice, but it's not enough. I want what's best for Sabrina, and I'm concerned that you won't be able to give her the life she deserves."*

Debra's gentle warning went unheeded as Steven pressed on, his words becoming more hurtful. *"You may have her captivated now, but it won't last. Mark my words, in a few years, she'll realize her mistake. You're not the right choice for her, Zayden."*

Sabrina could no longer contain her emotions. She pushed back her chair, her eyes glistening with unshed tears. *"Father, please, that's enough!"*

Standing abruptly, she turned and fled the room, leaving the others frozen in an uncomfortable silence. Zayden, his expression a mixture of concern and confusion, started to rise, but Steven held up a hand to stop him.

"Let her go, Zayden," Steven said, his voice gruff. *"She needs to understand that I only want what's best for her. This relationship is a mistake, and she'll thank me for it one day."*

Zayden's brow furrowed, his eyes darkening with a mix of anger and hurt. *"With all due respect, Mr. Chun, I believe it's Sabrina's decision to make. She's a grown woman, and she knows what she wants. Perhaps you should trust her judgment and respect her choices."*

Without waiting for a response, Zayden, too, left the dining room, his long strides carrying him quickly out of the mansion and onto the sprawling veranda. He scanned the grounds, searching for Sabrina, his heart heavy with concern and a lingering sense of rejection.

Finding her at the edge of the property, where a secluded bench overlooked the vast expanse of the Atlantic Ocean, he slowly approached, his presence announcing itself with the gentle crunch of gravel under his feet. Sabrina, her back to him, appeared engrossed in the mesmerizing dance of the waves below.

"Sabrina," Zayden said softly, his voice carrying a mixture of tenderness and apprehension.

Sabrina turned, her eyes red and swollen from unshed tears. She rose gracefully, her movements controlled despite the turmoil within. *"Zayden, I'm sorry you had to witness that. My father has strong opinions, and he can be very... vocal about them."*

Zayden closed the distance between them, his hands reaching for hers. *"It's okay. I understand family dynamics can be complicated. But I want you to know, I'm not going anywhere. Your father may not approve, but that won't change how I feel about you."*

Sabrina's eyes glistened with fresh tears as she stepped into his embrace, her body trembling slightly. *"Thank you,"* she whispered, her voice thick with emotion. *"But what if he's right? What if I'm making a mistake? What if we're not meant to be together?"*

Zayden held her tightly, his heart aching for the doubt that had been sown in her mind. *"He's not right, Sabrina,"* he murmured firmly. *"We belong together, and nothing will change that. Your father may have his concerns, but they're rooted in his own fears and expectations. We decide our future, no one else."*

Zayden cupped her face gently in his hands, his thumbs brushing away the stray tears that had escaped. *"Sabrina, look at me. You are more than enough. It's never been about money for me. It's about love, and we have that in spades."*

She sniffled, her brow creasing as she searched for reassurance in his eyes. *"But what about children? I want a large family, and I know that comes with financial responsibilities. I don't want to burden you or our future children."*

Zayden's eyes shone with a mixture of determination and adoration. *"We'll figure it out together, just like we've navigated everything else. Financial challenges are surmountable, but a lack of love and support can cripple a family. We have a strong foundation, and that's what matters most."*

Sabrina's lips curved into a tentative smile, her doubts beginning to melt away under the warmth of his unwavering love and acceptance. *"You really mean that, don't you?"*

Zayden nodded, his expression earnest. *"I do. And I'm willing to prove it, not just to you, but to your father as well. I may not be the man he envisioned for you, but I'll show him that I can provide for you and our future family in ways that matter."*

She stepped forward, closing the slight distance between them, and placed a soft kiss on his lips. *"Thank you,"* she whispered.

Zayden's arms tightened around her, his eyes reflecting the depth of his feelings. *" No matter what challenges we face, we'll face them together. Your father may not approve of me now, but I'll earn his respect, and more importantly, I'll keep earning yours every day."*

Chapter 26

As the sun set over Virginia Beach, the gentle ocean breeze carried a hint of salt and the promise of an enchanting evening. The lights of the boardwalk twinkled in the distance, providing a dreamy backdrop to the unfolding events. Sabrina and Zayden, their relationship tested by recent challenges, found themselves navigating a new phase in their journey of love and self-discovery. It was a critical juncture, and the presence of Emma, the insightful and caring producer of Will You Marry Me? added an element of guidance and support they both needed.

Emma arranged to meet the couples, aware that this stage of their relationships required a deeper exploration of their feelings and commitments. She understood the complexities that came with intense public scrutiny and the pressure to deliver captivating television. At a cozy beachside café, with the sound of waves providing a soothing backdrop, Emma initiated a heart-to-heart conversation.

"You're at a point now where you should be questioning the longevity of your marriages," Emma began, her voice laced with a gentle seriousness. *"It's normal to have doubts and worries. This experience is designed to test you, and how you respond to these challenges will define your relationships."*

Both couples nodded, absorbing her words and acknowledging the gravity of the moment. Emma's reminder that their journeys would be filled with obstacles served as a sobering realization, but it also ignited a spark of determination within them.

She proposed a dating challenge, designed to reignite the spark and strengthen their bonds. *"This challenge will push you to be creative, thoughtful, and intentional in your relationships. Remember, it's not just about the grand gestures, but also the little moments that build intimacy and connection."*

The dating challenge brought about varying results for the couples. While Victoria and Josh seamlessly adapted to the task, demonstrating a natural synergy, Sabrina and Zayden struggled to find their rhythm. Their attempts at rekindling romance felt forced and lacked the effortless connection that once defined them.

As the challenge progressed, Sabrina found herself questioning the nature of her relationship with Zayden. Was their connection more physical than emotional? Had her father's doubts about Zayden's ability to provide for her struck a chord? These thoughts ate away at her, casting a shadow over their once vibrant dynamic.

One evening, as Sabrina and Zayden prepared for a dinner party with Victoria and Josh, Sabrina's insecurities bubbled to the surface. She meticulously prepared a spread of homemade Mexican dishes, hoping to create a cozy and inviting atmosphere. As they sat down to eat, the aroma of spices and the sound of soft music filled the air, setting the stage for profound conversations.

"So, Victoria, how are things going with you and Josh?" Sabrina asked, a hint of uncertainty in her voice. She desperately sought reassurance that their relationship wasn't the only one experiencing growing pains.

"It's going really well," Victoria replied with a warm smile. *"We're taking things day by day, but I feel like we're on the same page most of the time. He even told me that he loves me."* She gave a shy glance at Josh, who returned her look with a loving smile.

Sabrina's heart sank as she turned to Zayden, her eyes searching for an unspoken confirmation that he felt the same way. Zayden, noticing her unspoken question, gave her a small smile, his eyes conveying a mixture of love and uncertainty.

"Zayden and I are..." Sabrina trailed off, unsure how to describe their current state. *"We're working through some things, I guess. It's been a little challenging lately."*

Victoria, sensing her friend's turmoil, reached out and placed her hand on Sabrina's. *"It's okay to have ups and downs. That's totally normal. Remember, this challenge is meant to test us. It doesn't define the strength of your relationship."*

Sabrina's eyes welled up with tears as she nodded. *"I know, but it's hard not to compare. Especially when you and Josh seem so sure of each other."* She paused, taking a steadying breath. *"Zayden hasn't said 'I love you' yet, and I can't help but wonder if my dad was right. Maybe we rushed into this."*

Victoria squeezed her hand gently. *"Don't be too hard on yourself, or Zayden. Love takes time, and it comes when you least expect it. For me, it was when I caught Josh writing furiously on his laptop. He later confessed that he was writing about us and how he felt. It was so sweet and unexpected."*

Sabrina dabbed at her eyes with a napkin, feeling a mix of emotions. She was happy for her friend but also envious of the certainty Victoria seemed to have found. She turned her gaze toward the deck, where Josh and Zayden stood, their silhouettes framed by the orange glow of the setting sun.

"Do you love him, Sabrina?" Victoria's question hung in the air, heavy with anticipation.

Sabrina hesitated, her eyes flitting between Zayden and Josh. She loved Zayden, but saying those words out loud felt like a daunting hurdle. *"I—I don't know,"* she admitted, her voice barely above a whisper. *"Maybe I'm just afraid to say it first."*

"There's nothing wrong with that," Victoria assured her. *"Love can be scary, but it's worth taking the risk. And if it's meant to be, it will happen when you least expect it."*

Meanwhile, on the deck, Josh and Zayden stood side by side, leaning against the railing as they gazed out at the crashing waves. The sun had dipped below the horizon, casting a warm glow over the ocean.

"I'm in love with Victoria," Josh said, his voice filled with a mixture of wonder and trepidation. *"I never thought I'd feel this way about someone, but she's changed everything."*

Zayden remained silent for a moment; his eyes fixed on the dancing waves. *"I really care about Sabrina,"* he finally said. *"She's an amazing woman, and I feel something strong for her. But I'm afraid to say 'I love you.' What if she doesn't feel the same way?"*

Josh turned to face Zayden, resting a hand on his shoulder. *"You won't know until you take that leap of faith. Love is a gamble worth taking. And besides, I think she feels the same way about you."*

Zayden sighed, his eyes reflecting the turmoil within. *"I'm also worried that we won't make it to the three-month mark. With everything going on, especially after seeing her parents, we've grown apart. Between work and the show, our relationship has taken a back seat."*

Josh nodded sympathetically. *"Then we need to step up our game. Let's plan a date for our ladies. Show them that we're still invested and that we care. We can't let this challenge defeat us."*

The dinner party concluded with a mix of emotions. While Victoria and Josh felt more confident in their connection, Sabrina and Zayden were left with a sense of uncertainty. However, the challenge had ignited a spark, and they were determined to fan the flames and rediscover the magic that had brought them together.

Chapter 27

The sun shone brightly over Virginia Beach as Zayden and Sabrina prepared for their date. It had been a while since they had some quality time just the two of them, away from the prying eyes of the cameras and the expectations of their families. Zayden, ever the enthusiastic planner, had suggested a day trip to the local theme park. It was the perfect opportunity to let loose and have some fun.

As they arrived, the energetic atmosphere enveloped them. The vibrant colors, thrilling rides, and aroma of delicious junk food created a delightful sensory experience. Zayden, with his broad shoulders and muscular frame, towered protectively over Sabrina as they navigated the bustling crowds. Her long dark hair flowed gracefully in the gentle breeze, contrasting with her delicate light beige skin.

They embarked on their adventure, laughing and holding hands as they braved the twisting, turning roller coasters. Zayden's deep voice reverberated with excitement as he encouraged Sabrina to confront her fears and join him on the most exhilarating rides. With each adrenaline-pumping twist and turn, their enthusiasm grew, their laughter filling the air.

Between rides, they indulged in a plethora of sinful treats. They munched on sticky candy apples, their mouths watering as the sweet, sticky syrup coated their tongues. Zayden playfully fed Sabrina cotton candy, the spun sugar dissolving on her tongue, leaving behind a burst of fruity flavor. They savored greasy, delicious fries and shared a giant pepperoni pizza, devouring it with their hands, uncaring of the mess.

As the day progressed, the sun dipped lower in the sky, casting a warm glow over the park. Zayden and Sabrina, their stomachs full and their faces glowing with contentment, decided to call it a day. Their feet were sore, their voices hoarse from shouting over the rides, but their spirits were high as they made their way back home.

The drive home was filled with lively conversation as they recapped their favorite moments of the day. Soon enough, they pulled into the driveway of their cozy abode. Stepping inside, they were greeted by the familiar comfort of their home. Their eyes met, and an unspoken agreement passed between them. It was time to continue their passionate exploration of each other.

Zayden wasted no time, pulling Sabrina close and crushing his lips against hers. His hands roamed her curvy body, igniting a fire within her. She responded eagerly, her hands tangling in his hair, pulling him closer. Their kisses became more urgent, fueled by the pent-up desire that had been building throughout their fun-filled day.

Without breaking their kiss, Zayden guided Sabrina toward the bedroom. He laid her gently on the bed, his eyes darkened with desire as he took in the sight of her tattooed lower backside and the glittering bellybutton ring that gleamed in the soft light. With slow, deliberate movements, he began to undress her, his hands shaking slightly with anticipation.

Sabrina's heartbeat quickened as Zayden revealed her soft, supple skin. She reached for his belt, eagerly unbuckling it and tugging at his clothes. Soon, they were both naked, their bodies pressed together, skin on skin. Zayden's hands roamed over Sabrina's delicate curves, his touch both possessive and worshipful.

He trailed kisses down her neck, his tongue tracing the delicate lines of her collarbone. His hands cupped her full breasts, thumbs brushing over her sensitive nipples, eliciting a soft moan from Sabrina. She arched her back, offering herself to him, her body responding eagerly to his touch.

With gentle fingers, Zayden explored every inch of her soft skin, memorizing her with his touch. His lips traveled lower, leaving a trail of fiery kisses down her stomach. He paused at her navel, teasing the piercing with his tongue before continuing his descent.

Sabrina squirmed with anticipation, her hands clutching the bedsheets as she felt Zayden's breath against her most intimate core. With gentle, probing licks, he tasted her, his tongue exploring her sweetness. Her hips bucked involuntarily as he found her clit, circling it with deliberate strokes that sent shockwaves of pleasure through her body.

"Oh, Zayden," she moaned, her hands gripping his hair, urging him on.

Zayden looked up at her, his eyes smoldering with desire. *"You taste so fucking good,"* he growled, before diving back in, his tongue relentlessly working its magic.

Sabrina's breath quickened as she neared the peak. Zayden's skilled tongue and eager fingers pushed her closer and closer to the edge. Her body tensed, every nerve alight with pleasure, and then she cried out, her release washing over her in waves. Zayden continued his ministrations, drawing out her pleasure until she was reduced to a trembling mess, her body sated, for the moment.

But Zayden wasn't finished with her yet. He wanted to pleasure her again, wanted to hear her cry out his name in ecstasy. He positioned himself between her legs, his hard length pressing against her entrance. With a slow, deliberate thrust, he slid inside her, filling her completely.

Sabrina gasped at the sensation, her eyes fluttering closed as she relished the feeling of being stretched around him. Zayden waited, giving her a moment to adjust to his size, before beginning to move. His hips circled slowly, his length stroking her in a tantalizing rhythm.

"Feels so good, baby," he murmured, his voice hoarse with desire. *"Wrap your legs around me."*

Sabrina complied, her legs locking around his waist, drawing him even deeper. Zayden began to move with purpose, his thrusts becoming harder, faster. The bed creaked in time with their passionate rhythm.

Their bodies moved in perfect sync, each meeting of their flesh sending sparks of pleasure through them both.

Sabrina's nails dug into Zayden's shoulders as she met his thrusts with her own urgent rhythm. The sensation was overwhelming, building inside her once more. She felt Zayden's breathing quicken, his body tensing as he neared his own release.

"Cum with me, baby," he groaned, his voice thick with need.

And as if on cue, they both tumbled over the edge together. Zayden roared her name as he emptied himself inside her, his body shuddering with the force of his release. Sabrina cried out, her walls clenching around him, her body shaking with the intensity of her orgasm.

In the aftermath, they lay tangled together, their sweat-slicked bodies still joined as one. Zayden nuzzled Sabrina's neck, placing soft kisses along her sensitive skin. She hummed contentedly, a smile playing on her lips as she threaded her fingers through his hair.

"That was..." Sabrina trailed off, searching for the right words.

"Incredible," Zayden finished for her, his voice a satisfied rumble. *"You're incredible."*

She turned her head to look at him, her almond eyes sparkling with affection. *"So are you."*

They shared a tender kiss, their lips moving gently against each other. In that moment, all the tensions and doubts that had plagued them recently faded away. This was why she had fallen for him—his ability to make her feel desired, his unrestrained passion, and the deep, unwavering love that bound them together.

With a contented sigh, Zayden pulled Sabrina closer, ready to drift off to sleep with her in his arms. Their passionate encounter had reminded them both of the deep connection they shared, and the unspoken promise of a future filled with love, laughter, and endless possibilities.

Little did they know, their journey together was far from over, and the next chapter of their lives would bring new challenges and unexpected twists that would test their love and strengthen their bond even further.

But for now, they savored the afterglow of their passionate reunion, content to let the future unfold as it may.

Chapter 28

The peaceful post-coital atmosphere was abruptly shattered by a desperate pounding on the apartment door, tearing Zayden and Sabrina away from their passionate reverie. The sudden intrusion startled them, but they quickly sprang into action, tossing on some clothes. Zayden, his face still flushed with desire, pulled on a pair of sweatpants, while Sabrina, her cheeks flushed with a mixture of embarrassment and concern, quickly slipped into some yoga pants and a baggy shirt.

As Zayden made his way to the door, his heart raced with a mixture of curiosity and apprehension. Pulling the door open, he was met with a sobbing Brittney, her model-like features distorted by anguish. Her eyes, rimmed with smudged makeup, pleaded with him to offer solace. *"Oh my God, Zayden, I didn't know where else to go,"* Brittney choked out between sobs. Her usually sleek brunette hair was tangled, and her trembling frame seemed smaller than ever. *"I'm so sorry to just show up like this, but I really needed—"*

Before she could finish her sentence, her words trailed off as fresh tears streamed down her cheeks. Sabrina, her heart going out to the distraught woman, pulled her into a comforting embrace, guiding her inside. Zayden, his protective instincts kicking in, closed the door behind them, ensuring they had a moment of privacy.

"Take a seat, Brittney. We're here for you. Now, tell us, what's going on?" Zayden asked, his deep voice gentle and reassuring.

Brittney took a shuddering breath, steeling herself to recount the evening's events. *"It's Billy,"* she began, her voice shaking. *"We got into a huge fight. I found out he'd been texting other women behind my back, and when I confronted him, he lost his temper and hit me."*

Zayden's eyes narrowed at the mention of Billy's name. He knew all too well the kind of man Billy Twine was—rude, unapologetic, and always looking out for himself. The thought of him raising a hand to Brittney made Zayden's blood boil.

"Are you hurt?" Sabrina asked gently, her nurturing instincts as a nurse kicking in. *"Do you need me to take a look at any injuries?"*

Brittney shook her head, her hand flying to her cheek, which still stung from the slap. *"I'll be bruised, but it's not too bad. I just couldn't bear to stay there another minute. I felt so foolish for not seeing his true colors sooner."*

Concern etched across Zayden's face, and he immediately pulled out his phone. *"We need to call Emma and the police. You don't deserve to be treated like this, and that jerk needs to answer for his actions."*

Just as Zayden was about to hit dial, a loud, aggressive knock reverberated through the apartment, making their hearts sink. They recognized that knock.

"That's Billy," Brittney whispered, her eyes widening with fear. *"Oh God, he must have followed me here."*

Zayden's protective instincts kicked into high gear. *"Stay here,"* he instructed, his voice leaving no room for argument.

As Zayden strode towards the door, Sabrina rushed to Brittney's side, taking her hand and giving it a comforting squeeze. They watched as Zayden pulled the door open, his broad shoulders filling the frame.

Billy stood there, his handsome features twisted with anger. His chiseled jaw was set, and his eyes blazed with a mixture of rage and humiliation. The sight of Zayden standing there, a barely concealed Brittney behind him, only served to fuel his fury.

"Brittney, get your ass out here," he snarled, his gaze darting past Zayden to where Brittney stood with Sabrina.

Zayden's stance was firm and unyielding as he replied, *"She's not going anywhere with you. Why don't you just leave, Billy? You've done enough damage for one night."*

Billy's muscular frame seemed to fill the doorway as he advanced, his gaze locked on Zayden with pure loathing. *"You stay out of this, Moss. This doesn't concern you."*

Zayden refused to back down. *"When it comes to a woman's safety, it concerns all of us. Now get lost before I call the cops."*

Billy's anger ignited at the threat, and he lunged forward, shoving Zayden with enough force to make him stumble backward. Without missing a beat, Billy swung, his fist connecting with Zayden's jaw.

Zayden, despite being caught off guard, quickly recovered. Years of playing football had honed his reflexes, and he easily dodged Billy's next punch, countering with a swift jab to the abdomen.

"You want to hit someone? I'll give you something to hit," Zayden taunted, a stark contrast to his usual laid-back demeanor. Years of being a football coach had kept him in shape, and his muscles were as strong as ever.

Billy snarled, his eyes wild with rage. He swung again, but this time, Zayden was ready. He grabbed Billy's wrist, twisting it behind his back and forcing him into a painful shoulder hold. *"Don't make this worse for yourself, man,"* Zayden growled. *"Just walk away."*

Billy, his face contorted with pain, struggled to break free, but Zayden's grip was like iron. Then, with a sudden surge of strength, Billy wrenched himself free, swinging wildly at Zayden. The two men grappled, fists flying, grunts and curses filling the air.

Suddenly, the sound of high-heeled footsteps echoed in the hallway, along with the distinct click of camera shutters. Emma, the show's producer, appeared, her eyes widening at the chaotic scene before her.

"Stop! Break it up, now!" she shouted, her voice cutting through the haze of testosterone.

The presence of the cameras seemed to snap Billy back to reality, and he abruptly ceased his attack, his chest heaving as he glared at Zayden. Zayden, too, realized the situation had escalated beyond what he'd intended, and he stepped back, his fists still raised, eyes burning with a mixture of anger and concern.

The police, who had been discreetly summoned by Emma, arrived on the scene, their sirens blaring. They took in the disheveled state of the two men and immediately recognized Brittney, knowing all too well the reasons for their visits to her home.

"Mr. Twine, you know why we're here," one of the officers stated, his tone leaving no room for argument.

Billy's shoulders slumped, his anger deflating like a punctured balloon. He cast a venomous glance at Brittney before being escorted away by the officers, his wrists cuffed behind his back.

Emma, her expression a mixture of concern and sympathy, guided Brittney to sit down, handing her a box of tissues. *"Are you okay? Do you need anything?"*

Brittney, her eyes red and swollen from crying, nodded, her voice hoarse as she whispered, *"I'm done with him. I can't believe I let myself fall for his charm. Thank you for being here."*

Sabrina, who had been watching the scene unfold with a mixture of fear and admiration for Zayden, approached him, her arms wrapping around his waist. *"Are you okay? That was crazy."*

Zayden, his heart still pounding, nodded, his arms instinctively reaching to pull Sabrina close. *"I'm fine. It's been a while since I got into a scuffle, but it's not my first fight."*

Sabrina's eyes searched his, her heart overflowing with love and concern. *"Thank you for protecting Brittney, and me. I know it's a lot to deal with, but I'm so grateful you're here."*

Zayden held her tightly, his heart warming at her words. He'd always been a protector, and in that moment, he felt more connected to Sabrina than ever before. But something was holding him back. The adrenaline of the fight was fading, and doubts were creeping into his mind.

"I love you," Sabrina whispered, her eyes shining with unshed tears.

Zayden's heart twisted at her words. He wanted to say it back, he truly did. But something was holding him back, a fear he couldn't quite name. He simply nodded, tightening his embrace as if his arms could convey what his words would not.

Sabrina pulled away slightly, concern etched on her face. *"Are you sure you're okay? I know it was a lot, but—"*

Zayden cut her off with a gentle kiss, silencing her worries, if only for a moment. *"I'm fine, really. Just a bit shook up. It's been an intense night."*

Sabrina searched his eyes, her own filled with a mixture of love and uncertainty. *"If you ever need to talk, I'm here. You know that, right?"*

Zayden forced a smile, his heart heavy as he pulled her close once more, seeking solace in her embrace. But his mind was turmoil, fear, and doubts swirling like storm clouds on the horizon.

Chapter 29

The sun had set, casting a warm glow over the room as Zayden and Sabrina found themselves entwined in a passionate embrace. The air between them crackled with intensity, their lips locked in a deep, hungry kiss. The taste of each other fueled their desire as they explored mouth and tongue, a primal hunger taking over.

Sabrina's hands roamed Zayden's sculpted chest, feeling the definition of his muscles as she began to grind her hips against his. She moaned into his mouth, her breath coming in short gasps as she felt his hard length pressing against her core. *"Oh God, Zayden... I want you inside me,"* she whispered, her voice thick with need.

Zayden's hands moved down to cup her round ass, giving it a firm squeeze before pulling her closer, their naked bodies pressing together. With a smooth motion, he entered her, filling her completely. Sabrina threw her head back, a mix of pleasure and ecstasy contorting her features. *"Fuck, yes... right there,"* she panted, beginning to ride him with slow, deliberate motions.

Their gazes locked, a fiery intensity burning in their eyes. *"You like that, baby?"* Zayden growled, his voice husky.

"Mmm, I love it," Sabrina replied, her eyes fluttering closed as she savored the sensation of his thick cock stretching her pussy. *"I love your cock inside me... it feels so good."*

Zayden's hands gripped her hips, guiding her movements as she picked up the pace. *"You're so fucking tight, Sabrina... I love your pussy wrapped around my dick,"* he grunted, his eyes rolling back in pleasure.

"I love you," Sabrina blurted out, her walls clenching around him as she spoke. *"Oh, fuck... I love you so much."*

Zayden's eyes snapped open, a brief moment of hesitation flashing across his face. *"Yes... just like that,"* he managed to reply, his voice hoarse.

Not getting the response she wanted, Sabrina slowed her hips, confusion and hurt clouding her features. *"Zayden... do you love me?"* she asked, her eyes searching his.

He swallowed hard, his Adam's apple bobbing as he tried to formulate a response. "Of course, I do... it's just—" he started, but Sabrina cut him off.

"Don't say 'it's just'," she interrupted, her voice laced with frustration. *"Don't make excuses. If you loved me, you'd say it without hesitation."*

With that, she slid off him, leaving him feeling exposed and vulnerable. *"Sabrina, wait... where are you going?"* Zayden asked, propping himself up on his elbows.

"It's nothing... I just need a minute," she replied, her voice wavering as she began to get dressed.

Zayden sat up, the sheet falling from his waist, leaving him naked and vulnerable. *"It's something,"* he insisted, his brows furrowed. *"Talk to me, Sabrina. What's going on?"*

With a heavy sigh, Sabrina turned to face him, her eyes holding a mix of emotions. *"I'm just... I don't know... I need some space, that's all,"* she said, not meeting his gaze. *"I think it's best we take a break from this... from us."*

"A break?" Zayden repeated, his heart sinking. *"What do you mean? We're married, Sabrina. We took vows."*

"I know, and I honor our marriage, but..." Sabrina trailed off, her eyes filling with tears. *"But you don't love me, Zayden. I can feel it. And I can't keep doing this if I don't know where your heart is."*

The truth of her words hit him like a ton of bricks. Zayden opened his mouth to speak, but no words came out. He searched for an explanation, but his usual charm and quick wit failed him.

Seeing his hesitation, Sabrina's hurt turned to anger. *"That's what I thought,"* she said, zipping up her jacket. *"I'll be staying at Victoria's tonight. It's for the best... at least until we figure out what we really mean to each other."*

"Sabrina, wait!" Zayden called out, but it was too late. The door slammed shut, leaving him alone in the bed they had just shared so passionately.

Zayden collapsed back onto the pillows, his hands running through his hair. *"What the fuck just happened?"* he muttered to himself. How had the most incredible night of passion taken such a sharp turn?

His mind raced back to the moments before, when Sabrina had confessed her love. He had felt something shift inside him—a realization that he, too, was falling hard for this incredible woman. But the words *"I love you"* had always carried a weight for him, a commitment he didn't take lightly. And now, as he lay there in the aftermath of their argument, he realized he had let his fear of those three simple words drive a wedge between them.

Cursing under his breath, Zayden swung his legs off the bed and stood up, his bare feet padding across the floor as he moved to the window. He watched as Sabrina's car disappeared down the street, a hollow feeling settling in the pit of his stomach.

"I fucked up," he whispered, the weight of his mistake pressing down on him. He knew that Sabrina, with her conservative upbringing, valued commitment and stability above all else. And now, he feared he had shattered the trust and connection they had so carefully built.

As the reality of the situation sank in, Zayden's initial frustration turned to determination. He refused to let this be the end. He loved Sabrina—he knew that now with a certainty that shook him to his core. And he would do whatever it took to win her back and prove that his love was real.

The coming days would be a test of his resolve and his ability to express his true feelings. Zayden knew that winning back Sabrina's heart would require more than just words—it would demand actions that demonstrated his love and commitment.

As he stood there, naked and vulnerable, Zayden's heart pounded with a mix of emotion: the sting of his mistake, the intensity of his love, and the burning desire to prove to Sabrina that he was the man she could trust with her heart.

Little did he know that fate had more surprises in store for them both, and the path to reconciliation would be anything but smooth. But Zayden was determined to persevere, to show Sabrina that their love story was far from over... it was just getting started.

And so, as the moonlight cast a soft glow over the quiet street, Zayden's mind raced with plans to win back the woman who had stolen his heart, knowing that the greatest challenge—and reward—lay in proving that his love for Sabrina was forever.

The future held uncertainty, but one thing was clear: Zayden would not rest until Sabrina was back in his arms, their love stronger and more enduring than ever before.

Chapter 30

The sun was setting over Virginia Beach, casting a warm glow across the city as Zayden Moss lounged on his couch, absorbed in reviewing footage from his high school football practice. The familiar rhythms of the game offered him a comforting escape from the tumult of his personal life, particularly his complicated relationship with Sabrina Chun. In the kitchen, a pot of marinade simmered on the stove, filling the air with mouthwatering aromas as he awaited Sabrina's return.

However, his tranquil evening was abruptly interrupted by a knock at the door. Puzzled, Zayden rose from the couch, wondering why Sabrina would knock since she had a key. As he pulled the door open, his confusion turned to surprise at the sight before him. Standing on the threshold was Yolanda Green, her curvaceous figure accentuated by her designer clothing. She exuded an air of uncertainty, her eyes downcast as she hesitantly met Zayden's gaze.

"Hey, Zayden," she murmured. *"Can we talk?"*

Zayden's curiosity got the better of him, and he stepped aside to invite her in. As they settled on the couch, the scents from the kitchen continued to waft through the apartment, a savory backdrop to the unfolding conversation.

Yolanda immediately launched into a tirade about her woes with Xavier, her voice laced with frustration and disappointment. Zayden listened attentively, his eyes darting occasionally to the television screen, where the football game continued to play silently in the background.

"I just don't know what to do anymore, Zayden," Yolanda sighed, running a hand through her hair. *"Xavier and I are just not on the same page. It's like we want different things from life."*

Zayden nodded sympathetically, his thoughts turning to his own relationship trials. *"I know how you feel, Yolanda. Things with Sabrina and me aren't exactly smooth sailing right now either."*

Yolanda's eyes widened in curiosity. *"Really? But you two seemed so solid. What's going on?"*

Zayden hesitated, choosing his words carefully. *"It's complicated. I still haven't told her that I love her."*

Yolanda's eyes narrowed in disbelief. *"Why not? What are you waiting for?"*

A pained expression crossed Zayden's face as he struggled to articulate his fears. *"I'm scared, Yolanda. Scared of getting hurt. We've only got three months left on the show, and I'm afraid that once it's over, she won't want to be with me. I mean, look at me. I'm broke, I'm a teacher, and I'm not exactly what her parents envisioned for her."*

Yolanda shook her head, a faint smile playing on her lips. *"Zayden, are you that naïve? What you and Sabrina have is special. It's more than just lust or physical attraction. It's a deep bond that some people search their whole lives for and never find. Don't sell yourself short."*

Her words struck a chord, and Zayden felt a pang of guilt for not expressing his love for Sabrina sooner. *"I guess I've just been scared of taking that leap,"* he admitted. *"But you're right. Sabrina and I have something unique, and I don't want to lose it."*

Yolanda's expression softened, and she reached out to place a comforting hand on his arm. *"Then don't let her go, Zayden. Sabrina is too good to let walk away. Fight for her."*

Zayden nodded, feeling a surge of determination. *"You're right. I won't give up on us."*

As they sat there, a comfortable silence enveloped them, the unspoken understanding hanging heavy in the air. Zayden felt a connection with

Yolanda, a shared humanity in their struggles with love. In that moment, he felt grateful for her presence and her wisdom.

Without warning, their tranquil moment was shattered by the sound of the apartment door opening. Zayden and Yolanda turned to see Sabrina standing in the entryway, her eyes widening in shock at the scene before her. Zayden's heart sank as he realized the potential for misunderstanding.

Yolanda, sensing the sudden shift in the atmosphere, quickly rose from the couch, her face a mask of embarrassment. *"Oh my god, Sabrina. I'm so sorry. I didn't realize you'd be back so soon."*

Sabrina's eyes darted between the two of them, her face a storm of emotions. *"Zayden, we need to talk,"* she said, her voice shaking.

Before Zayden could respond, Yolanda stepped forward, her eyes filled with apology. *"Sabrina, please let me explain. I came here to talk to Zayden about my relationship issues, and we were just—"*

But Sabrina held up a hand to silence her, her eyes welling with tears. *"No, Yolanda. It's fine. I understand."* With a heavy heart, she turned to Zayden, her expression a mixture of hurt and anger. *"But I thought we were past this, Zayden. I thought I could trust you."*

Confused, Zayden stood, his hands raised placatingly. *"Past what, Sabrina? Nothing happened, I swear. Yolanda just needed someone to talk to."*

But Sabrina wouldn't be consoled. The memories of her previous relationship, tainted by infidelity, clouded her judgment. *"I know what I saw, Zayden. Afterwhat I've been through, I can't help but feel like I'm being played for a fool again."*

Yolanda interjected, her voice desperate. *"Sabrina, please. You have to believe me. Zayden would never do that to you. He loves you."*

At her words, Zayden's head snapped towards Yolanda, his eyes wide with surprise. It was the first time he had heard her utter those words, and they hung heavy in the air between them.

But Sabrina was impervious to Yolanda's pleas. With a final, heartbroken glance at Zayden, she turned and walked out of the apartment, her steps heavy with grief.

Zayden's heart sank as he realized the depth of Sabrina's hurt and misunderstanding. Without a moment's hesitation, he sprinted after her, calling her name.

In the hallway, he found her, her back against the wall, shoulders shaking as she struggled to contain her tears. Zayden's heart broke at the sight of her pain, a pain he felt partially responsible for.

"Sabrina, please let me explain," he pleaded, his voice filled with desperation. *"Nothing happened between me and Yolanda. I would never cheat on you. You have to believe me."*

But Sabrina's wounds were fresh, the scars of her past still raw and tender. *"How can I, Zayden? I've been down this road before. I trusted my last partner, and they betrayed me. I can't go through that again."*

Zayden's eyes blazed with sincerity. *"I'm not them, Sabrina. You have to understand that. I would never hurt you intentionally. Yolanda and I were just talking. She needed my support, and I gave it to her as a friend. That's all."*

Sabrina's eyes, red-rimmed and glistening, searched his face, seeking any sign of deception. *"I want to believe you, Zayden. But it hurts, seeing you with someone else. It brings back all the pain and insecurity."*

Zayden's heart went out to her, and he took a tentative step forward, reaching out to cup her cheek. *"I know it does, Sabrina. And I'm sorry for that. But I love you, and I would never do anything to jeopardize what we have. Please, try to forgive me for this misunderstanding."*

His words, laced with raw emotion, struck a chord deep within Sabrina. She wanted desperately to believe him, to trust that their love was strong enough to withstand this storm.

"I want to, Zayden," she whispered, her voice thick with unshed tears. *"But it's hard. I need time to process this and heal."*

Zayden nodded, understanding clouding his eyes. *"Take all the time you need, Sabrina. I'll be here, waiting for you."*

With a final, yearning glance, Sabrina turned and walked away, her steps heavy with the weight of her conflicted emotions.

Zayden stood there, his heart heavy with love and regret, watching the woman he loved walk away. He knew he had to give her space and time to heal, but the wait felt like an eternity.

Chapter 31

The sound of Yolanda's raised voice echoed through the hallway, reaching Sabrina's ears as she sat on the couch, tears streaming down her face. Victoria stood at the door, her hand on the knob, preventing Yolanda from entering and witnessing Sabrina's vulnerable state. The tension between the two women was palpable, as the situation had escalated far beyond a simple misunderstanding.

Sabrina's heart ached as she heard Yolanda's words, her emotions raw and exposed. She had sought refuge at Victoria's apartment, hoping to find solace and support from her friend after the tumultuous events of the past few days. The confrontation with Zayden, the confusion, and the pain of his hesitation to reciprocate her love still weighed heavily on her mind. Now, with Yolanda's unexpected arrival, Sabrina felt her world crumbling further.

Yolanda's piercing gaze met Victoria's, her frustration evident. *"Let me talk to her, Vic. I need to set things straight,"* she pleaded, her voice filled with determination. Victoria, sensing the urgency in her tone, reluctantly stepped aside, allowing Yolanda to enter.

Yolanda's eyes immediately locked onto Sabrina, who sat with her head bowed, her shoulders shaking with suppressed sobs. The sight of her friend in such distress stirred a mix of emotions within Yolanda. She had not anticipated finding Sabrina in such a state, and her heart softened, momentarily forgetting their differences.

"Sabrina, I need to talk to you," Yolanda said, her voice softer now, devoid of the previous anger. *"I know you're hurting, but please listen to me."*

Sabrina lifted her head, her almond eyes red and swollen from crying. She stared at Yolanda, her expression a mix of hurt and confusion. *"What do you want, Yolanda? I don't think there's anything left to say,"* she whispered, her voice hoarse from crying.

Yolanda took a deep breath, her eyes pleading with Sabrina to understand. *"I know you think I had something going on with Zayden, but I swear, nothing happened between us. We just talked. I told him about my relationship issues with Xavier, and how I wasn't sure if we were meant to be."*

As Yolanda spoke, Sabrina's eyes widened in disbelief. *"You told him that? You told Zayden you and Xavier weren't working out?"* she asked, her voice laced with astonishment and a hint of anger.

Yolanda nodded, her gaze steady. *"Yes, I did. And I'm telling you this because I don't want you to throw away a good thing. You have a great man, Sabrina. A real catch. Do you know how hard it is to find a good black man these days?"*

Sabrina's eyes narrowed, her face contorting into a scowl. She was not in the mood for Yolanda's unsolicited advice, especially when it came to her relationship. *"Is that all you have to say? You're here to lecture me about finding a good black man? I thought we were friends, Yolanda, but I guess I was wrong."*

Yolanda's eyes flashed with hurt, but she maintained her composure. *"I'm not here to lecture you, Sabrina. I'm trying to help. I know what it's like to be in a complicated relationship. I've been through my fair share of heartache. But Zayden... he's different. He's a good man, and he loves you. Don't let your insecurities ruin what you have."*

Sabrina shook her head, her tears flowing again. *"You don't understand, Yolanda. It's not just about insecurities. Zayden didn't say he loved me back. He hesitated, and it broke my heart. I can't just ignore that and pretend everything is fine."*

Yolanda's expression softened, and she took a step closer to Sabrina. *"I know it's hard, but sometimes love isn't always easy. Maybe Zayden needs time to process his feelings. He's been through a lot, and he might not be ready to fully open up yet. But that doesn't mean he doesn't love you."*

Victoria, who had been quietly observing the exchange, spoke up. *"Yolanda might have a point, Sabrina. Zayden is a complex guy, and he's been dealing with his own issues. Maybe you should give him some time and space to sort through his feelings."*

Sabrina wiped her tears, her eyes darting between Victoria and Yolanda. She knew they were trying to help, but the pain was still fresh, and she couldn't bring herself to forgive Zayden so easily. *"I don't know... I just feel so lost. I thought I had found the one, but now I'm not so sure."*

Yolanda's eyes glistened with empathy. *"I know it's confusing, but sometimes love requires patience and understanding. If you truly love Zayden, give him a chance to prove himself. You two have been through so much together, and I believe you can overcome this."*

Sabrina took a deep breath, her mind racing with conflicting thoughts. She wanted to believe Yolanda and Victoria, but her heart was still guarded. *"I'll think about it,"* she said, her voice barely above a whisper. Yolanda nodded, her eyes filled with relief. *"That's all I ask. Just give him a chance, and talk to him. Don't let this misunderstanding come between you. You're stronger than that, Sabrina."*

With that, Yolanda turned and walked towards the door, her footsteps echoing in the hallway. Victoria followed her, leaving Sabrina alone with her thoughts. The apartment fell silent, and Sabrina sat motionless on the couch, contemplating her next move.

The encounter with Yolanda had stirred up a whirlwind of emotions within Sabrina. On one hand, she felt a sense of anger and betrayal, as Yolanda had indeed crossed a line by discussing her relationship with Zayden. But on the other hand, there was a glimmer of hope in Yolanda's words. Perhaps Zayden did need time to process his feelings, and maybe their love was worth fighting for.

As the minutes ticked by, Sabrina's mind wandered back to the moments she had shared with Zayden. The laughter, the passion, and the connection they had built over the past few months. She thought about their honeymoon, their date at the theme park, where they had ridden the thrilling roller coasters, sharing screams of excitement and joy. She recalled the multiple intimate nights they had spent together, exploring each other's bodies and discovering new depths of pleasure.

But then, the memory of Zayden's hesitation crept in, casting a shadow over her thoughts. The moment he had failed to reciprocate her love, the confusion and pain that had followed. Sabrina's heart ached as she realized how much she had invested in this relationship, and the thought of losing Zayden terrified her.

Determined to make a decision, Sabrina stood up, her resolve strengthening. She knew she couldn't run away from her feelings, nor could she ignore the potential for love to blossom again. With a newfound sense of purpose, she reached for her phone, her fingers trembling as she dialed Zayden's number.

As the phone rang, Sabrina's heart pounded in her chest. She took a deep breath, steeling herself for whatever lay ahead. After a few rings, Zayden's deep voice answered, his tone cautious and unsure.

"Hello?"

Sabrina's voice cracked as she spoke, her emotions threatening to overwhelm her. *"Zayden... it's me, Sabrina. I... I need to talk to you."*

There was a moment of silence on the other end, and then Zayden's voice, filled with relief and concern. *"Sabrina, I'm so glad you called. I've been thinking about you nonstop. Can we meet? I need to explain things to you."*

Sabrina's heart raced, and she nodded, even though Zayden couldn't see her. *"Yes, I want to meet."*

Chapter 32

The sun had just begun to rise over Virginia Beach, casting a warm glow on the city as Sabrina made her way to Zayden's apartment. Her heart was heavy with uncertainty, the events of the past few days playing on a loop in her mind. The confrontation with Zayden, the unexpected appearance of Yolanda, and the subsequent revelations had left her feeling confused and vulnerable. As she approached the familiar building, she took a deep breath, steeling herself for the conversation she knew was inevitable.

Zayden, unaware of Sabrina's arrival, was still lost in his thoughts. He sat on the couch, his eyes fixed on the wall as if searching for answers within the blank canvas. The previous night's events had left him shaken, and he couldn't shake the feeling of impending loss. He had made a mistake by not being honest with Sabrina sooner, and now he feared the consequences of his hesitation.

As Sabrina entered the apartment, the sound of the door caught Zayden's attention. He turned, his eyes widening at the sight of her. She stood there, her eyes brimming with unshed tears, her body language tense and uncertain. Zayden's heart sank, knowing that this moment would determine the fate of their marriage.

"Hey," he said, his voice hoarse with emotion. *"How are you feeling?"*

Sabrina took a moment to compose herself, wiping away a stray tear that had escaped. *"I'm not sure how I feel, to be honest,"* she replied, her voice quivering slightly. *"I've been thinking a lot about us, about our marriage."*

Zayden's stomach clenched at her words. He stood up, taking a step towards her, wanting to close the distance between them. *"What is it that you're thinking, babe? Talk to me."*

Sabrina took a deep breath, her gaze steady on Zayden. *"I'm questioning our marriage, Zayden. I can't help but feel that something is off. I saw Yolanda here, alone with you, and it brought back memories I'd rather forget."*

Zayden's eyes softened, and he took another step forward, reaching out to touch her arm gently. *"Nothing happened, Sabrina. I swear to you. Yolanda came to me for advice, that's all. I would never do anything to hurt you."*

Sabrina shook her head, her eyes filled with pain. *"It's not about what happened or didn't happen. It's about trust, Zayden. I've been cheated on before, and I can't bear the thought of going through that again. I don't want to get hurt, not by you."*

Zayden's heart ached as he saw the hurt and vulnerability in her eyes. He wanted to take away her pain, to assure her that he would never cause her harm. *"I would never cheat on you, Sabrina. You have to believe me. I love you, and I would never do anything to break your trust."*

Sabrina's eyes widened at his declaration, and she took a small step back, as if his words had caught her off guard. *"You... you love me?"* she whispered, her voice barely audible.

Zayden's throat constricted as he realized the weight of his words. He had never said those three words to anyone before, but in that moment, he knew they were true. *"Yes, I do. I love you, Sabrina Moss. I've been an idiot for not telling you sooner, but I was scared. Scared of getting hurt, scared of commitment, but I can't keep running from my feelings anymore."*

Sabrina's gaze softened, and for a moment, Zayden saw a glimmer of hope in her eyes. She took a step towards him, her hand reaching up to touch his face. *"You're really not lying to me?"*

Zayden captured her hand in his, pressing a gentle kiss to her palm. *"Never, my love. I'm not lying, and I never will. I want to be with you, only you. Please, don't leave me, don't divorce me. I need you, Sabrina."*

As Zayden pleaded, Sabrina's heart melted. She could see the raw emotion in his eyes, the vulnerability he rarely showed to anyone. She knew in that moment that he was telling the truth, that his love for her was real. Her doubts began to fade, replaced by a surge of desire and love for this man who had captured her heart.

"I love you too, Zayden," she whispered, her voice breaking. *"I've been a fool for not seeing it sooner. I was so scared, but I can't deny my feelings anymore. I want to be with you, to make this work."*

As her words sank in, Zayden's eyes sparkled with unshed tears of relief and joy. He pulled her into his arms, holding her tightly as if he would never let her go. *"Thank you, Sabrina. Thank you for giving me another chance. I promise to make it up to you, to show you how much I love you every day."*

Sabrina smiled, her heart swelling with happiness. *"You don't have to prove anything, Zayden. Just love me, and I'll do the same. We can work through this together."*

Zayden's lips found hers in a passionate kiss, their mouths moving in perfect harmony. He tasted the sweetness of her lips, the warmth of her tongue as it danced with his. His hands roamed over her body, exploring the curves he had grown to love. He cupped her breasts, feeling her nipples harden under his touch, and she moaned into his mouth, encouraging him further.

Sabrina's hands were equally busy, unbuttoning his shirt to reveal his muscular chest. She traced the tattoos on his skin, her fingers lingering on the intricate designs. Zayden's breath quickened as she tugged at his pants, her hands slipping inside to grasp his hardening cock.

"I want you, Zayden," she whispered against his lips. *"Right here, right now."*

Zayden needed no further encouragement. He lifted her in his arms, carrying her to the bedroom in a rush of desire. He laid her gently on the bed, his eyes devouring her as he took in her beauty. Sabrina's long dark hair spilled across the pillows, her light beige skin glowing in the morning light.

He kissed her passionately, his hands moving to the hem of her shirt, lifting it over her head. Her breasts, full and perfect, were exposed to his hungry gaze. He lowered his head, taking a nipple into his mouth, sucking and teasing it until she arched off the bed, her back bowing with pleasure.

Sabrina's hands tugged at his pants, freeing his throbbing erection. She grasped his thick cock, her fingers stroking the length of him as she whispered words of encouragement. *"I want to feel you inside me, Zayden. Please, make me yours again."*

Zayden couldn't resist her any longer. He positioned himself between her legs, his cock nudging at her entrance. With one smooth thrust, he filled her, their bodies joining as one. Sabrina gasped, her eyes fluttering shut as she adjusted to his size.

"You feel so good, baby," he murmured, his voice rough with desire. *"So tight and wet. I love being inside you."*

He began to move, his hips thrusting in a steady rhythm. Sabrina met his movements, her body rising to greet each powerful stroke. Zayden's hands gripped her hips, guiding her as he plunged deeper, their bodies moving in perfect synchronization.

"Yes, Zayden, harder," she panted, her nails digging into his shoulders. *"Fuck me harder, please."*

Zayden obliged, his pace increasing as he slammed into her, their bodies slapping together with each thrust. The room filled with the sounds of their passion, their moans and cries echoing off the walls. Zayden's eyes never left Sabrina's face, watching as she surrendered to the pleasure he was giving her.

"I'm close, baby," she whispered, her voice strained. *"Make me come, Zayden."*

Zayden felt his own climax building, his balls tightening with each thrust. He wanted to give her everything, to show her how much he loved her with his body. He quickened his pace, his cock plunging deep, hitting her sweet spot with every stroke.

"Cum for me, Sabrina," he grunted, his voice hoarse. *"Let me feel you squeeze my cock."*

Sabrina's body tightened around him, her pussy clenching and releasing as her orgasm claimed her. Zayden felt her muscles milk his cock, and with a final, powerful thrust, he emptied himself into her, his seed filling her depths.

They lay entangled, their hearts racing and their bodies glistening with sweat. Zayden brushed the hair from Sabrina's face, his lips finding hers in a tender kiss. *"I love you, Sabrina Moss. Always and forever."*

Sabrina smiled, her eyes sparkling with love and contentment. *"I love you too, Zayden Moss. I'm so glad I chose you."*

As they lay in each other's arms, the morning sun streaming through the window, they knew that their love had survived the test of doubt and misunderstanding. Their marriage, though young, was stronger than ever, and they were ready to face the world together, confident in the power of their love.

Chapter 33

The cameras were rolling, capturing the intimate moment between Zayden and Sabrina, as they sat across from Emma Rand, the producer of the reality TV show, 'Will You Marry Me?'. The bright studio lights illuminated the couple's nervous yet determined faces, a stark contrast to the calm and collected Emma. This was the moment of truth, the culmination of their three-month-long journey on the show.

"So, Zayden and Sabrina," Emma began, her voice warm and soothing, *"we've witnessed your love story unfold, from the initial sparks to the recent challenges. It's been a rollercoaster, to say the least. Now, we've reached the final decision point. The question remains, will you choose divorce or marriage?"*

Zayden, his muscular frame tense with anticipation, reached for Sabrina's hand under the table. He gave it a gentle squeeze, seeking comfort and strength from his partner. *"We've been through a lot these past few months,"* he started, his deep voice echoing in the quiet studio. *"There were times when I thought we wouldn't make it, but our love kept us going. It's been a wild ride, and I'm not ready for it to end."*

Sabrina, her dark eyes shining with emotion, nodded in agreement. *"Our journey hasn't been easy, but it's been worth it,"* she said, her voice steady and confident. *"We've faced misunderstandings, doubts, and even my parents' skepticism about our relationship. But through it all, Zayden has shown me a love I never thought possible."*

Emma leaned forward, her expression curious and compassionate. *"Can you tell me, Zayden, what made you hesitant to commit to Sabrina in the beginning? What changed your mind?"*

Zayden took a deep breath, his broad shoulders rising and falling. *"I guess I was scared,"* he admitted, his voice softening. *"I've had my heart broken before, and I didn't want to risk getting hurt again. But Sabrina is unlike anyone I've ever met. She challenges me, supports me, and loves me for who I am. I realized that love is a risk worth taking."*

"And Sabrina, you've been through a lot, especially with the pressure from your parents to find a suitable partner. What made you decide to take a chance on Zayden?" Emma probed further.

Sabrina's face softened as she recalled her journey. *"My parents have always had high expectations, and I wanted to please them. But I also wanted to find my own happiness. Zayden is... different. He brings excitement and spontaneity into my life. He understands me in a way no one else does. I realized that love is about taking a leap of faith, and I'm glad I took that leap with him."*

Emma smiled, her eyes glistening with genuine happiness for the couple. *"It's beautiful to hear how you've both grown and overcome your fears. And now, the moment we've all been waiting for. Zayden and Sabrina, what is your final decision?"*

Zayden and Sabrina exchanged a look, a silent communication filled with love and understanding. *"We choose marriage,"* they said in unison, their voices strong and resolute.

The studio erupted in cheers and applause as the crew celebrated this heartwarming moment. Emma stood up, her face beaming with pride and joy. *"Congratulations, Zayden and Sabrina! I'm so happy for you both. It's been a pleasure to witness your love story, and I wish you all the best for your future together."*

As the cameras continued to roll, capturing the raw emotion of the moment, Zayden and Sabrina embraced, their hearts overflowing with love and relief. *"Thank you, Emma,"* Zayden said, his voice hoarse with emotion. *"This show has changed our lives. We've grown so much, and we're ready to take on the world together."*

Sabrina added, her voice trembling slightly, *"I never imagined I'd find love like this. Zayden, you've shown me a new way of living, full of adventure and passion. I can't wait to start our married life and create a future filled with love and happiness."*

Emma's eyes twinkled with delight as she congratulated them once more. *"Well, I have no doubt that your future will be bright and full of wonderful surprises. Now, before we wrap up, any final thoughts you'd like to share with our viewers?"*

Zayden grinned, his playful nature returning. *"I just want to say, love is a crazy, beautiful thing. It can be scary, but it's worth fighting for. And Sabrina, I can't wait to spend the rest of my life with you, driving you crazy and making you smile."*

Sabrina laughed, her eyes sparkling with love and mischief. *"And I can't wait to drive you crazy right back, Zayden. Our love is a wild ride, and I'm ready for every twist and turn."*

As the interview came to a close, the cameras followed Zayden and Sabrina as they left the studio, hand in hand, their hearts filled with a newfound sense of hope and joy. The bright lights of the TV set faded into the background as they stepped out into the bustling city of Virginia Beach.

"What's the first thing you want to do now that the cameras are off?" Zayden asked, his eyes twinkling with mischief.

Sabrina arched an eyebrow, a playful glint in her eyes. *"You know what I want to do,"* she replied, her voice laced with anticipation.

Zayden's laughter filled the air, his deep voice resonating with joy. *"Your place or mine?"*

"Yours," Sabrina said, a smile playing on her lips. *"Besides, after our passionate reunion, I want to start planning our future together. I have a feeling our lives are about to get even more exciting."*

Zayden's smile widened, his heart swelling with love and pride. *"Our place, huh? I'm glad you've come to appreciate my humble abode. But I have a feeling it's not just the house that's keeping you around."*

Sabrina's cheeks flushed with a hint of pink, her eyes sparkling with mischief. *"Well, I have to admit, there are certain... advantages to your place. But I'm also thinking about our future family. I can see us raising our children there, starting a new chapter of our lives."*

Zayden's eyes widened in surprise, his heart skipping a beat. *"Our children? You mean..."*

Sabrina nodded, her expression filled with love and excitement. *"Yeah, I'm pregnant. It's still early, but I wanted you to be the first to know. I think our love has created something truly special, and I can't wait to begin this new journey with you."*

Zayden's breath caught in his throat as he processed this life-changing news. He pulled Sabrina into a tight embrace, his heart overflowing with joy and gratitude. *"I love you, Sabrina. I can't believe we're going to be parents. This is the best surprise ever."*

"I love you too, Zayden," Sabrina whispered, her voice filled with emotion. *"I can't wait to see what the future holds for us. Our love has brought us this far, and I know it will carry us through the challenges and joys of parenthood."*

As they stood there, wrapped in each other's arms, Zayden and Sabrina felt a sense of peace and contentment wash over them. The past few months had been a whirlwind of emotions, but their love had persevered, growing stronger with each test. Now, as they embarked on a new chapter of their lives together, they knew that their bond would only deepen as they faced the joys and challenges of marriage and parenthood.

The sun shone brightly on the happy couple as they strolled through the vibrant streets of Virginia Beach, their hands clasped tightly together. Zayden and Sabrina's love story was far from over; it was just beginning, and they couldn't wait to write the next chapter, filled with love, laughter, and the unexpected surprises that life had in store for them.

As they made their way home, Zayden and Sabrina's minds raced with excitement and anticipation. They knew their lives would never be the same, and they embraced the unknown with open arms, ready to face whatever the future held for them, as long as they faced it together.

Don't miss out!

Visit the website below and you can sign up to receive emails whenever Michael Gordon publishes a new book. There's no charge and no obligation.

https://books2read.com/r/B-A-KEXRC-JYQFF

BOOKS 2 READ

Connecting independent readers to independent writers.

Also by Michael Gordon

Will You Marry Me?

About the Author

Michael Gordon is a modern romance author who enjoys writing steamy, heart racing, interracial romances. When he's not writing, he's reading other swoon worthy interracial romance stories, traveling with his wife & kids, or watching sports.